Beginners' Guide to Fake Marriage

Benna Bos

*Note: This is a massively re-written version of the 2024 self-published work “Just Marry Her” by the same author under a different pen name, L.R. Martiny.

Print ISBN: 979-8-9960477-0-3

Cover Art by: Lyssa from Booked Forever Shop
Cover Designer: Bos Consultancy and Publishing

www.bennabos.com

ACKNOWLEDGEMENTS

This book has had a long journey. It started as a submission to a pretty famous publishing house that shall remain unnamed. That house was interested in the bones of the story but said that people don't want to read about dogs. I know what you're thinking; I thought the same thing. And I was like, well, I guess I'm not publishing with them, because what is life without dogs? Anyway, I self-published the book under a different pen name, but I eventually realized that I had more work to do on the story to really bring out its heart. So I pulled it and began a massive re-write. Thanks to my incredible beta readers—Nadia Smith, Mae Todd, Eline Evans, and Megan Wiliolo—I found the core of this story and brought it to the front. Then, my amazing copy editor and proofreader, Mandolyn Tracy, polished up the manuscript. And finally, the incredibly talented Lyssa from Booked Forever drew the cutest image for me to use on the cover. I am eternally grateful to them all because writing this fun, beach read brought me joy, and now I get to share that joy with all of you.

Chapter 1

Make a Good First Impression

The strength of five dogs, ranging in size from a feisty Chihuahua to a rambunctious Husky, was more than Missy's relatively small body could handle. That the dogs were attached to a thin piece of leather dropped over her shoulder like the cross-strap of a purse from hell only made her balance that much more tenuous as she struggled to keep up with them.

Sandals slipped wildly on her feet as she worked to stay upright. She knew it was useless to fight the wave of motion dragging her forward. Resistance would only result in her being dragged like a sack of flour.

Any attempt to steer the direction of the pack of dogs was also out of the question; there was a very real possibility that she would end up face down on the sandy beach of St. Croix, wishing she'd never boarded the plane from San Francisco.

The dogs stopped long before they reached the sloppy ocean waves. The husky and the bulldog made the executive decision to veer hard left, taking the smaller dogs and Missy with them. But the sharp turn was too much for the flimsy sandals Missy wore.

She went down.

As her face plant created a reverse sand sculpture, the leash strap shifted so the attachment point pulled hard at her shoulder. The dogs yanked at the leash wildly, making her feel a bit like a fish at the end of a line.

The tugging suddenly stopped. She registered the click of the metal clasp being removed from the strap of death clinging to her frame. The blessed sound was followed by that of a woman's voice.

"Come here, sweeties. Now sit. Stay."

Missy planted her palms in the sand and pushed herself up to her knees in the most graceful move she could manage. The dogs sat or lay on the sand in various poses. But none of them were in a hurry anymore. It seems they had reached their destination.

A pair of long legs clad in dark blue jeans stood in front of the regimented canines. Above a light brown leather belt, a deep gray button-down blouse, pressed and starched, featured tiny brown dogs in various orientations. A regal chin, sharply angled cheek bones, stark hazel eyes, and unruly curls made up the striking appearance of a woman Missy would know anywhere.

She pulled herself to standing and held out a dusty hand. "Hi, um, Ms., um…" Missy racked her brain. What had Uncle Jack said? Don't call her Ms. Adams, just call her Quincy. "Quincy. Ma'am."

Quincy's striking eyes slowly moved as if they were roaming Missy's form. She was pretty sure Quincy was cataloging her dirt covered sandals and dusty bare calves. When she put it on that morning, Missy had appreciated her choice of light-yellow tank dress, but now she feared it may not meet Quincy's expectations.

If Quincy was disappointed, she didn't let on. "No 'ma'am', please." She held out her hand. "Nice to meet you. Are you Jack's niece?"

Missy tried to remember everything she'd ever been told about shaking hands. Don't grip too hard. Grip hard enough to let them know you are a strong person. Let them choose the grip. It resulted in her pumping her hand against Quincy's as if she were trying to give CPR to her palm.

Quincy wrangled her hand free of Missy's bizarre grip. "So, Jack's niece?"

"Yes, ma…Yes. I'm Missy Greenwood. Your new assistant."

"I saw your resume. It looks good. Just finished a training program. Had a mentor for the last year. Worked with two-dozen clients." She nodded her head. "It all indicates a good start to your career."

The words were said without a hint of sarcasm, and two things hit Missy at once: one of the most famous dog trainers of all time had memorized her resume; and Missy had arrived in front of her like a pure amateur being dragged by dogs as if she were a ragdoll. She couldn't decide which emotion was on top—pride or humiliation.

"I'm excited to be here, working with you." Missy glanced around at the set up. Camera's perched in several locations around the beach, people moving across the sand with purpose. "Um… What should I do?"

Jason, the set assistant who'd handed Missy the dogs, hadn't been very explicit. He'd just told her to take the dogs over to Quincy. Missy had been on the job less than ten minutes, and she wasn't entirely sure what the hell she was supposed to do now that she'd delivered the dogs to the show's star.

"We're going to shoot some quick scenes with these five." Quincy waved at the animals that had attempted to murder Missy but were now completely chill at Quincy's feet. "Since it's your first day, why don't you just hang out and watch? We'll take a break in a bit." Quincy glanced at the dogs. "And then you and I can take them back to the play yard."

Missy stepped away from Quincy, keeping the cameras

in sight as she traversed the filming area. She had no idea what their peripheral vision was, but she no intention becoming part of an accidental photo bomb. It wasn't until a wave lapped across her sandals that she realized she'd gone too far. She shifted enough to stay out of reach of the water and stood there on the beach—just inches from the serene waves—wringing her sweaty hands.

Quincy was magic in front of the cameras, working with the five disparate dogs Missy had brought her. In today's episode of *Dogs in Paradise*, she was dealing with "stay," a command that would have been immensely helpful a few minutes ago.

The brilliance of the show's premise was that Quincy could showcase basic training principles on the constantly rotating groups of dogs that came through her specialized board and train facility. People clamored for the opportunity to get their dog into Quincy's program so their pup could learn new skills and be featured on the popular television show, all while their parents got to vacation on the island.

As she watched, Missy reflected that real-life Quincy was everything on-television Quincy appeared to be. There were very few additional takes demanded by the director. There were no tricks, like additional people wrangling the dogs between takes; Missy was never called in to help out. There were no shortcut methods of training that made the dogs behave out of fear and pain. None of that. Not a single disillusionment. Quincy was nothing short of amazing.

Still in full fangirl mode by the time filming took a break for lunch, Missy loped forward and reached for the dog leashes. But Quincy only handed her three, keeping the leashes of the troublesome husky and the bulldog herself. Missy oscillated between guilt over not being able to do her job and awe as both dogs perfectly heeled at Quincy's side while they walked along a small, dirt path.

When they crested the hill, Missy's breath caught in her throat. Stretching out ahead of her was Quincy's estate. In the foreground, the play area for the dogs shone fresh and green. The large, fenced-in patch of grass was at least the size of half a baseball field. It sat beside a freshly painted, wood-sided barn so brilliantly red it looked like the nose of a circus clown. A few hundred feet further on sat a quaint, single-story house painted a rich, butter yellow, and trimmed in white. The entire estate perched on a hill above a sandy beach, framed with intense aquamarine water that sparkled in the midday sun.

Quincy extended her arm toward the scene. "It's a hell of a spot, isn't it?"

Missy nodded her head and managed to squeak out, "Yeah, it is."

"I inherited it from my mother's family, and everyone else in my generation with claim to it wanted to stay in the states, so it's all mine. I'm very lucky."

They reached the play area, which was separated from the rest of the property by a white, wooden fence. Quincy swung the gate open and easily unclipped the dogs in her care while Missy wrestled with her three.

After an epic struggle that pitted Missy against the unruly furballs, she managed to let the dogs loose so they could romp in the play area with the others. Quincy waved at a pretty, young woman who sat on a bench in the middle of the yard, a giant bowl of water at her feet and a treat pouch attached to her belt. Quincy shut the gate behind her and gestured to Missy with a 'come hither' motion.

Missy followed her across the stretch of space between the play yard and the house. Her sandals provided no protection from the native grasses that scratched the sensitive skin on the tops of her feet and slashed across the bright purple polish coating her toenails. When they reached a cream-colored door at the front entrance, Quincy opened it, without using a key, and held it for Missy. The bright smile decorating Quincy's face sent spikes of an unnamed sensation through Missy's gut.

Missy ducked her head as she passed by her host, the scent of lilacs and leather kissing her nose. Past the door, the open space afforded a full view of the coziest little cottage Missy had ever seen.

Her family had a few cottages—one in the Sierras, one in Tahoe, and one buried in the Redwoods just north of San Francisco. But they were really just small houses nestled into great places. They held the same clean, sterile lines, fashionable furniture, untouchable paintings, and uncluttered surfaces as the Green family's main residence. None of those supposed cottages had the sweet, homey feel of this place.

Shiplap lined one wall of the enclosed living room. Exposed beams loomed overhead. As they moved past the floor-to-ceiling bookshelves and the fluffy sectional sofa, Missy's feet coasted across polished hardwood floors that, while cared for, still showed the bumps and bruises of a life well lived.

Her gaze jumped from one painting to another. The walls were splattered with them. Not so many as to crowd the space, but certainly more than one per fifty square feet as her mother allowed. All of them looked experimental, colorful, intense, and connected to one another in an inexplicable way.

Missy followed Quincy through a set of bar doors, and they plunged into a spectacular kitchen covered in sandstone tiles and wooden counters. The centerpiece was an island the size of a kayak with a set of gleaming stainless-steel cookware hanging over it like stalactites dripping graciously over a cave floor.

"Do you have any dietary restrictions?" Quincy asked.

"I'm a vegetarian."

Quincy smiled. "Me, too. Actually, I'm a pescatarian. I don't do it often, but I will eat fish. Can't lie about that. I guess you could say I'm an aspiring vegetarian. Did Jack tell you that?"

Missy nodded. She really needed to say something more substantial than the three words she'd uttered so far in this house. But she was so deeply star struck she couldn't seem to get her shit together. After eight hours on a flight the day before as well as one sleepless night—all of it spent planning exactly how she would act around Quincy Adams and what she would say—she still stood there unable to utter a single sound.

Quincy pulled open the refrigerator door, fished out several items, and hefted them over to the island. She glanced at Missy after dropping her haul in the center of the massive counter. "Sit down."

Missy wanted to argue, to offer to fix lunch herself. She was the assistant after all. But she wasn't sure how to go about it. Instead, she planted herself on a barstool, saddled up to the counter, and watched as Quincy began unwrapping everything. A red pepper emerged, along with a container of rice, some diced green onion, fresh cilantro, and heirloom tomatoes. Moments later, Quincy was bent over, shoving stuffed peppers into the oven.

When she was done, she stood on the opposite side of the counter from Missy, her hands dropped on the granite countertop. She fit perfectly into the wood and stone environment surrounding her. Dog hair clung to the cuff of her shirt. A dark blonde curl hung over her temple. It was like watching a movie character come to life. "So, how do you like the island?"

"I haven't seen much of St. Croix yet. I just got in last night. I'm staying at my uncle's place."

Quincy spun around suddenly and grabbed two glasses from a cupboard. She filled them with water before sliding one to Missy. "That's too bad. I think everyone should get a little time to adjust before they are plunged into a new job."

"Uncle Jack said it was an emergency, that your last assistant left kind of suddenly?"

Quincy chuckled. "Yeah. It was sudden. He fell in love with a passenger on a cruise ship that came to the island. Sixteen hours later, he hopped aboard and headed for Fort Lauderdale with a forty-year-old tech tycoon."

"Wow."

"Yeah. Well. I always say follow your dreams." Quincy smiled. "Anyway, it wasn't an emergency. I have great staff that run the kennels. That was Gabriela we saw out at the play yard. I will properly introduce you when we pick up the dogs. I have two other staff as well, Luis and Anton. Between the three of them and myself, we're doing okay." Quincy's expression changed suddenly. She stuck a hand out toward Missy. "Not that I'm not happy you're here. I am."

Missy shoved a hunk of dark hair over her shoulder. "No, I get it. I mean, I know it's only because my uncle is the producer, but I'm so grateful to be here." The reason she almost didn't come. Using her prominent family connections had always been on her "don't" list. But this was one opportunity she'd been unable to turn down.

Quincy was midway to taking a sip of her water when she changed course and plopped the glass on the granite countertop so hard water sloshed over the edge. A few drops escaped to land on her thumb. “Not true. The show wouldn't have hired you if I didn't approve. I looked at your resume and your training tapes. You may be green, but that's perfect for this job.”

Uncle Jack had said exactly the same thing to her, only she didn't quite believe him at the time. Now it was coming from Quincy herself. Missy needed to know more. “Why's that?”

Quincy leaned over on the counter, propping herself up on her elbows. “After the first three seasons of my show, I discovered that there were basically two kinds of people who desperately wanted the training assistant job. The first were people who had no experience, were super excited about learning the trade because it looks good on television, but when it came to actually having to train a dog, they wanted to take the easy way.” Quincy frowned. “I don't do the easy way.”

Missy nodded. She didn't jump in and tell Quincy she didn't believe in harsh methods in dog training either. Quincy had seen her materials and would know Missy was a positive methods trainer. And yeah, it was harder. Teaching is always harder than terrifying.

“Then there are those with experience. Too much experience. They want a show of their own. And maybe some of them deserve it, but either way they aren't content to assist me on my show. But you.” She pointed her finger at Missy. “You're perfect. Good experience and eager to learn more.”

Missy nodded. She'd said almost exactly that in the interview recording she'd sent. She couldn't believe Quincy had paid so much attention to her and actually wanted her here. If she could melt from sheer joy, she'd be a puddle at the base of the stool she sat on.

Somehow, Missy managed not to disintegrate into a

mass of fangirl goo during lunch. She did not, however, stop herself from audibly moaning when she tasted the stuffed peppers Quincy made. She also couldn't manage to keep the smile off her face as they loped back over to the play yard.

Apparently all twenty-four visiting tourists' dogs that were being boarded for training were now out and romping around. Between Missy, Gabriela, and Quincy, they needed to extract the same five dogs they'd had before lunch from the pile of playing puppies.

Missy was assigned to capture Mitsy, the Chihuahua. Which should have been easy. But little Mitsy was fast. Her tiny legs dodged and swooped. At one point, Missy was sure she had her. Her waiting hands were just about to close around that petite little waist when Mitsy ducked under one of the raised dog beds beneath the shaded area near the barn.

Embarrassment filled Missy as she glanced up to check on the others. Gabriela stood calmly by the gate, both the Boston terrier and the schnauzer attached to leases and sitting dutifully at her feet. Beside her, Quincy had both the husky and the bulldog literally eating out of her hand.

Her gaze locked with Quincy for a brief moment before she looked away. Quincy didn't say a word. Instead, she crouched down and held out her free hand. And wouldn't you know it, that damn Chihuahua ran over and hopped right into her arms.

****

Uncle Henry frowned at his beloved grill. "Would it be a problem if your veggie burger accidentally touched my full meat burger?"

Missy cringed, then straightened her spine and

plastered on a smile. "Not one bit, Uncle H."

Missy admired Henry's confident stance in front of the grill, one hand raised, brandishing his spatula as if it were a weapon, the other firmly planted on his hip. Despite wearing shorts of questionable length, a Hawaiian button-up shirt that strained at the middle, and a pair of worn flip flops, Henry stood like he was about to enter the Met Gala.

"So glad you're here, kid." Uncle Jack hugged her from the side, squeezing so hard she nearly spilled her beer. "We haven't gotten to spend enough time with you in the past couple of years."

She poked him in the ribs, her finger pressing into the side of his deeply worn Nirvana t-shirt. "That's because you and Henry missed the big family ski trip last winter."

"Yeah. But we were on the family reunion cruise last summer, and you missed that." He poked her back.

She had missed the cruise because she'd been steeped in her dog training class at that time and didn't want to take ten days off, even for her lovely, exasperating family. Also, she wasn't big on boats. That was a whole other thing.

"How was your first day of work?" The grill was only steps away from the table in their quaint, flower-stuffed garden, so it was easy for Missy and Jack to hear Henry's question.

The white paint on the iron table looked fresh, and she ran her hand over the surface as she answered her uncle. "I was a disaster, but I think the job is great."

"So you couldn't catch a Chihuahua. So what?" Jack said.

"How do you know about that?"

Jack smirked. It was a talent of his. He was a blue-ribbon smirker. Mom once told her that when Jack was in middle school, his principal made their parents sit through a two-hour long meeting about Jack's facial expressions. Missy couldn't for the life of her figure out how Nana and Papa managed that without breaking down into hysterics.

"No, seriously. How do you know?" When she got nothing from that uncle, she turned to the other one. "Uncle H?"

"I'll tell you, sweetheart." Henry waved the giant spatula in the air. "There are cameras on the play yard and the kennels."

"What?" Missy whipped her head around to stare at Jack. He just smirked again.

Henry pointed the spatula at his chest. "I put them there myself."

Henry didn't work for *Dogs in Paradise* like Jack did. But he was the island's best electrician. So it shouldn't have been a surprise that he did some set-up work for his husband's show.

"I guess I better watch myself when I'm in the play yard."

Uncle Jack raised an eyebrow. "Are you planning on doing something naughty in the play yard?"

Missy poked him again. "I don't know, I might want to make out with Gabriela. She's really something. Guess if I want to, we'll have to sneak behind the barn."

Henry laughed as he slipped an overflowing paper plate in front of Missy. The veggie burger perched on a massive bun with a mound of fixings that forced it to lean like the Tower of Pisa. A mountain of potato salad threatened to spill out onto the table.

"Okay," Uncle Jack said. "So the young kennel assistant is hot. But what did you think of Quincy?"

She contemplated taking a massive bite of burger so she didn't have to answer. But that was only a delay tactic. And it would only poke the bear and make both her uncles that much more intrigued.

She shrugged. “She seems great.”

“She is great.” Henry stuck another plate in front of Jack before sitting down across from them both. “I bet she’ll be the best boss you’ve ever had.”

“Actually.” Jack hefted his burger. “I’m Missy’s boss. She works for the show, not for Quincy’s dog training business, which is technically separate.”

“Well, in that case… good luck, kid.” Henry hefted his beer toward her. Missy laughed and clinked her own bottle with his before taking a swig.

She was happy to be here on this beautiful island with her loving and hilarious uncles and a dream job. If only she could keep her shit together around the dog trainer she admired, everything would be fine.

****

Day two wasn’t going much better than day one. So far, Missy had managed to let Mitsy loose, resulting in a hair-raising chase around the filming set that nearly upended a very expensive camera setup. She’d also spilled coffee all over her white blouse. The bright side of the coffee spill was that her top now matched her splotch-design skirt.

But Quincy never so much as made a face at her. She just smiled sweetly each time they made eye contact. Between the smiles, the total tolerance of Missy’s rookie mistakes, and the lunch she’d made her on her first day, Missy was developing a serious crush on Quincy that went beyond respect for her talent as dog trainer.

“Hey, Missy. Come here,” Landry called.

Missy loped over to where Landry and Jason stood beside the camera Mitsy had tried to take out earlier.

"What's up?"

Jason smiled at her. Which was kind of nice since he hadn't said more than six words to her since she'd arrived on set. He was apparently the senior-most crew person and took that position very seriously. Landry, however, had been nice to Missy from day one, asking her how she was doing after her humiliating spill in front of Quincy. They had even greeted her this morning with a fresh cup of coffee. She was glad that the staff on set was warming to her; she lived in fear of being seen as nothing more than the spoiled niece of the boss.

"Help us settle a bet," Landry said.

How she could help them with anything on day two was a total mystery, but she was willing to play along. "Sure. What do you need to know?"

"When you were at Quincy's for lunch yesterday, did you see any pictures of her and a woman?"

Missy thought she'd done a good job of paying attention to Quincy before getting this job. She'd watched every episode of the show and followed Quincy's social media, but she was obviously missing some tea. "I think I saw some family pictures. A mom and maybe a sister or niece."

"No, this would have been real relationship stuff, you know?"

"I don't remember seeing anything like that. Why?"

"Huh." Jason hooked a thumb in the belt loop of his jeans and glared at Landry. "I guess you win."

Landry grinned. "I sure do."

"Wait. You have to tell me what's up."

Jason turned away, fiddling with a cord leading to the camera. But Landry looped an arm around her shoulder. "I'll tell you."

She and Landry walked slowly away from Jason and

the set. Landry moved into the shade of a massive tree, gripped Missy by her shoulders, and pulled her in front of them. "Quincy had a long-term relationship with Gina Bebeck, you know the actress that's been all the rage since she starred in that television show. I can't remember what it was called, but she played the hot, smart one."

Missy knew who Gina Bebeck was but didn't think she was quite as big a deal as Landry was making her out to be. "I remember her. I guess I didn't know they were together, though."

"Oh yeah. And the break up was a big deal. Gina basically made sure everyone knew about it. She plastered all this cryptic shit on socials about how awful she felt. Just enough to imply that everything was Quincy's fault without any concrete evidence. Then she started sending out all these quotes about people that are emotionally unavailable. It gave major bitter ex vibes."

Missy's stomach flipped as empathy flooded her. She knew what it was like to be on the wrong side of bad publicity and to feel helpless to do anything about it. "What did Quincy do?"

"Nothing. She basically disappeared from social media for a minute, and when she came back on, everyone was pretty sure it wasn't actually her, but someone she paid to do her socials. It was just off, you know?"

"I guess I didn't notice. When did all this go down?"

"This was before Quincy left the show in L.A. and moved out to the Virgin Islands to start *Dogs in Paradise*, so four years I'd guess."

"Did you work for her in L.A.?"

"Yeah, other than Jason and your uncle, I'm one of the few originals. I moved out here when Quincy did. I mean, she never said a word about Gina, but you know it's a bad break-up when you move your entire life and start a new business on an island to get away."

"But the show was pretty small before, and now it's huge. So the move was also a good business decision, right?"

Landry frowned at her, probably taking offense at the implication that the show had once been less than successful. Before she could offend them any further, she moved the conversation back to the original subject. "So, why were you and Jason betting on the photos in Quincy's house?"

"We were betting on whether or not Quincy was still hung up on Gina. Gina has been claiming lately that Quincy is calling her nonstop."

"Claiming how? Do you talk to her?"

Landry scrunched up their nose and stared at Missy like she'd said the dumbest thing they ever heard. "No. On socials. On blogs, and even in interviews with influencers. She's been blowing up Callie McNally's comments section."

"What the hell is a Callie McNally?"

They waved a hand at Missy. "Never mind. The point is, for people who pay attention to celebrity gossip—which you clearly do not—it's everywhere that Quincy and Gina might get back together. Largely because people think that Quincy is basically begging Gina to take her back."

"This all sounds a little ridiculous to me. And frankly, none of our business." Landry's mouth dropped open, and Missy realized she's just lost her chance to make friends. Maybe it wasn't too late to save face. "What I mean is, I don't think Quincy is holding a candle for Gina. I didn't see any pictures of them in her house. And I think you're right, that would have been a big clue."

Landry's demeanor shifted, and their face lit up.

"Exactly. That was what I was saying. I don't think Quincy's interested at all, but Jason buys into Gina's drama. So I told him that pics in the house would be a good tell. We'd been in the house before but it's been a while, and since you were just there yesterday for lunch, we figured you could settle the bet for us." They grinned. "And you did."

Landry slung their arm around her, and the two of them walked back toward the set together. Missy was thrilled to be on the inside with the crew, and not all that mad that maybe Landry was right about Quincy's love life.

Chapter 2

Assess Your Motives

Six days ago, Missy entered Quincy's life. It was a little weird that she knew the precise number of sunrises and sunsets that had passed since the moment her new assistant landed at her feet in a puddle of pups.

Quincy had anticipated the arrival of Jack's niece as she had any other new staff person on the show or at her training and boarding business—with high hopes and a healthy dose of reserved skepticism. But she noticed Missy in a way she never had with anyone else who was even remotely close to being in her employ. Seeing Missy in her sassy sundresses, the hem flirting around her knees, the thin knit hiding nothing, created a host of unwanted thoughts racing through Quincy's head.

She needed to tuck away her desire and avoid being alone with Missy like they'd been in her kitchen that first day. It was a long-established tradition for Quincy to feed lunch to the new hires on their first day. But never before had the event been so awkward.

As solid as the plan was to never have Missy in her home alone again, it had already gone awry. Today, she'd invited Jack to join her lunch break, hoping to pick his brain about a few things, but he'd shoved Missy at her, saying that he and Henry had something to celebrate and Missy needed a place to be. Then he waggled his eyebrows and disappeared.

So she ended up walking back with Missy and the dogs

to the play yard. On the way, she tried to think of the best possible lunch to make that was both quick, easy, and would leave the least amount of time for staring at Missy's smiling face across the table.

As they gathered the dogs and began the walk back across the property, she decided she would make a stir fry. She had fresh vegetables she'd just picked up at the local market yesterday, and she could make that sauce that she'd made for her kennel staff last week. They'd gushed about it for days.

Cresting the hill, Quincy spotted a fancy sports car outside her house, and everything, including her mental menu rundown, came to a complete stop. She planted her feet in the dirt path at the junction. To her right was the play yard, to the left her house.

Missy, preoccupied with trying to get Hank and Ike to heel, missed the sudden change, and her nose slammed into the space between Quincy's shoulder blades.

Quincy whirled around. "Are you okay?"

Missy held her head with one hand while the other jigged and bobbed in an attempt to keep control of the leashes attached to Hank and Ike. Quincy snapped her fingers and gave the dogs a sit command. Both dogs sat, their bodies relaxed, tongues lolling as they stared up at Quincy, no doubt hoping for a treat.

Quincy placed her fingers gingerly on Missy's wrist, pulling her hand away from her face. "Let me see."

Missy's liquid brown eyes struck Quincy. A wave of sensation rushed through her from head to toe. Quincy moved her gaze to Missy's nose. The skin was red, but there was no blood, no sign of any serious damage. "Let's get you some ice. We'll just take the dogs to the house." She reached out and gently extracted the leashes from Missy's hand.

She headed toward the house, sighing as she once again caught sight of the reason she'd been startled into a stop to begin with—the high-end luxury automobile parked in front of her home. She'd recognize it anywhere. It was clean and shiny because it was lovingly stored with a local shopkeeper who was paid to care for it. It remained in his garage for all but the four times a year its owner came to the island from the mainland.

Quincy swore under her breath and headed back down the path. They looped around to the back of the house where Quincy ushered Missy and the dogs into the tile-lined mudroom. They wiped puppy paws and unclipped leashes. Quincy opened the painted white door and let the dogs loose into the main part of the house. Hank and Ike, who very much played off each other's energy, both bounded into the living room. It only took them a moment to locate the basket of toys that sat beside the couch.

Leaving the dogs to their play, Quincy turned to face her own fate. Standing between the living room and kitchen like a roadblock was a short, intense woman with long, black hair, bright red lipstick, and a pair of sparkly, rhinestone-lined, cat-eye glasses. "Hi Myra."

"Well, hi there." Myra's overly cheerful greeting included a long, thirsty look at Missy. "Who's this?"

Quincy stopped a few feet from Myra. Missy, who seemed to be tethered to Quincy by an invisible line, stood to her side. "Myra, this is my new training assistant, Missy. She started last week. Missy, this is Myra, she's my agent and she's been an unfortunate part of my life for many years now."

Myra threw her head back dramatically and laughed. Quincy rolled her eyes. Myra was nothing if not a sucker for a pretty face. She wasn't about to hide it either. She stretched one hand out to Missy, probably mentally popping the buttons of Missy's blouse. "It's a pleasure to meet you." She took her gaze off Missy just long enough to address Quincy. "Q, I can't believe you didn't tell me you had a new assistant."

Quincy stepped around the greeting and headed toward the kitchen. A part of her wanted to tell Myra to knock it off, but it wasn't her place. Maybe Missy was charmed by Myra's overt flirtations. And all the better if she was, because Quincy didn't need the headache of feeling attraction to her own assistant.

"The show hired her, not me. I didn't think it was something you needed to know. Besides, I thought you were tied up on the mainland." Quincy rounded the corner of her kitchen island and headed straight for the cupboard. By the time she turned back around with three glasses perched between her hands, Myra was walking in her direction, one hand placed on Missy's lower back.

She glanced at Missy, who looked just as comfortable as she always did. Better to check though. "Myra, don't touch the young person you just met, please."

"Fair enough. Sorry, Missy. I'm just a friendly lady."

Quincy made a noise from the back of her throat.

"No, it's fine." Missy slid onto a barstool. "And I'm not that young."

"Oh." Myra slid onto the barstool beside her. "How old are you?"

"Seriously, Myra? How rude are you?"

Missy smiled. "It's okay. I'm twenty-six. I'm a little green at the dog training thing because I got my degree in something else and spent a couple years floundering at doing that before I found my passion."

Quincy wanted to know more. The resume she'd seen for Missy only included the dog training work, nothing else. But this wasn't the time to dig into Missy's past.

Instead, she set the glasses on the island in a neat row and went to the refrigerator. "What are you doing here, Myra?"

"I just got in and wanted to check on you."

Quincy pulled out a tall, glass pitcher of homemade lemonade and slid back to the counter with it. "I'm good." She spoke to them both, but her smile was for Missy. When she gazed at her she remembered her nose. "Oh shit." She hustled back to the freezer and busied herself with getting together an ice pack while Myra started quizzing Missy about where she was from and how she liked St. Croix.

By the time Quincy had gotten the ice pack on Missy's face, poured three lemonades, and stuck a bowl of pretzels out on the counter, Myra had dragged a miniscule amount of information out of the shy Missy. The facts amounted to her uncle having gotten her the job, she was excited to be here, and she grew up in San Francisco.

"Do you miss San Francisco?" Myra asked.

Missy shook her head awkwardly as she held the ice pack to her nose. "Not yet. The island is amazing."

"It is. I come up for a few weeks at a time. I have a couple clients here." Myra raised her eyebrows. "I live in L.A., but I go to San Francisco often. Maybe we met when I was there. Though I probably would have remembered."

Quincy found Myra only mildly amusing, most of the time she was deeply irritating. But Myra was family, distant relative or not, and if her mother was in fact watching over her, she'd be furious if Quincy found a less obnoxious agent to replace Myra.

"Okay, Casanova." Quincy said. "Lay off for a minute."

Myra chuckled. "You're just jealous of my moves.

Hey, speaking of which, did you think about what we discussed?"

Quincy shifted her gaze to Missy. Her eyes were wide with curiosity. She'd been that way from the beginning—always eager to learn more, know more, but hesitant to ask. Quincy offered up the information freely. "I have someone who does my social media for me."

Missy nodded as if this explained Myra's entire statement, which of course it didn't.

Apparently, Myra wanted to be in on the whole 'explain stuff to Missy' project, and she plunged in. "And this one." She pointed at Quincy. "Has a major problem."

Missy moved the ice pack off her nose to gape at Myra. "What kind of problem?"

"She's single."

"That's right." Quincy lifted her glass. "And I intend to keep it that way." Swearing off relationships had been easier than she realized when she'd fled L.A. and escaped to the Virgin Islands. She had no intention of plunging back into an emotional hellscape to deal with the current issue.

"Why is that a problem?" Missy asked.

"It's not," Quincy said.

Myra pressed her lips together, and her gaze moved from Missy to Quincy and back again. Quincy could put a stop to what Myra was about to say. Would probably do so if anyone else from the show was sitting here. The last thing she needed was for her business to be aired. Though in so many ways it already was. So she turned her attention to gathering vegetables and let Myra say whatever she wanted.

"She's got a bit of an image problem at the moment. Let's just leave it at that. And I think being in a committed relationship with lots of cute pictures and hearts and flowers, and all that jazz, would really help."

Quincy dropped a red pepper on the cutting board and started slicing it with clean movements. "That can't be the only way to deal with a shitty ex, Myra."

"It's not. But do you really want to end up on Dateline?"

Quincy couldn't help but laugh. Missy, on the other hand, still wore a confused expression. "My ex is the mysterious issue, Missy. She's mildly famous, and apparently, she's been teasing that we are getting back together."

"Are you?" Missy asked.

Quincy abandoned the red pepper and pulled out the onion, giving it a hard whack to the center to split it in half. That felt good. "No. I didn't move to an island in the Caribbean to get back together with my toxic ex."

"So," Myra said. "We need to get her off Quincy's back."

"Again," Quincy pointed the knife in Myra's general direction before realizing what she was doing and lowering it. "There has to be other ways. Couldn't we just deny it?"

"Already did. Made the whole thing worse. People were speculating that you were this pathetic scorned lover practically begging her to take you back."

"Ugh." Quincy hated that everything had gone so wrong with Gina. When she first broke up with her, she felt guilt over ending the long-term relationship. But these days Gina was making her wish they'd never dated in the first place.

"The way I figure it, you need to get out there. Go to a couple clubs, or out on a blind date or two. I know a few nice women."

"No you don't."

"I know a few women. Anyway, we can get you dates."

"But I don't want to date." Quincy said it like it was a manifesto, and in a way it was.

"Well." Myra threw her hands in the air. "Then I guess you have to get married."

And that was it, right there—the moment a crazy plan began to form in Quincy's head.

****

It had been twenty-four hours, and the idea Quincy had first grasped onto had only grown; now it whirled around in her head like a hurricane headed for landfall. And what the hell was with that inappropriate dream she'd had as soon as she'd finally fallen asleep?

The magic of coffee dripping eloquently into her mug could not chase away the images. Her mouth crushing against Missy's soft lips. Her hands roaming over Missy's hips, sliding further down.

Quincy shook her head violently. Could she fling the images away, tossing them into the trash can perched at the end of the kitchen island? Apparently not. And that is exactly why she had to push away any idea of asking Missy to help her with her miserable social media love life problem.

She reached for her laptop. She would bury herself in planning for the day's shoot. She would do what she always did when her mind refused to give her peace, occupy it with work until it had no choice but to let go of what plagued her. If that didn't work, she could call Olivia. But summoning her best friend was a last resort. She wasn't ready for the stark honesty that would require. Trying to ignore everything from her off-the-wall idea to her blossoming attraction to Missy was the better option.

She'd barely managed to open all the documents she needed when the chime of the doorbell echoed through the cottage, bouncing off the pine walls and skipping through the space. She ignored the tightness in her chest as she made her way to the front door.

Quincy swung the door open, and her breath dropped out of her in relief. "Jack."

"Hey, Quincy. Sorry for just dropping by."

He always said that, but it never seemed to actually stop him from doing it. Apparently, Jack had a moral objection to calling before he came over.

Quincy moved aside and held the door for Jack as he stepped into the foyer. "What's up?"

Jack strolled into the house and swung around, the rubber of his sneakers squeaking on her recently polished wood floor. "I wanted to talk to you candidly before we got started today."

Candid conversations never led to anything good. They were usually the harbinger to deep trouble that penetrated the very root of her life. Candid conversations had led to breaks ups, family fights, and even a firing once. It's why she avoided them like the plague.

"Um, sure." She folded her arms over her chest, closing herself off.

Jack swung his own arms wide like a circus ringmaster welcoming her to his tent. "Tell me. How's my niece doing?"

What probably seemed like an innocuous question to Jack caused a spike in Quincy's blood pressure. "Good. Really good. You want some coffee?" She moved past him and marched toward the kitchen.

Jack kept up with her, step for step. "Sure. But I need more than that."

She swung around the island and busied herself with filling a mug, then procuring both cream and sugar, since she knew Jack took his coffee with a lot of additives.

Jack dropped onto a barstool opposite her. "I mean, really. How's she doing?"

Quincy kept her gaze on the porcelain mug as she slid it across the granite countertop toward him. "I think she's just as good as we thought she would be when we agreed to have her come to the show. She's got a lot of talent and potential."

"I think so, too."

"Then why are you asking me if you already know?"

"She won't take my word for it. She thinks I'm biased. And the truth is, I am. That kid has been my favorite since the first time I held her. In my eyes, she's perfect." He shrugged. "But she says she started off on the wrong foot. Something about dogs gone wrong. And when I asked if things were better, she said she wasn't sure. So I woke up this morning with the intense need to know, really know, that she's doing well. I can't let her fail. And I don't want to have brought her here and set her up to fail."

"Jack." Quincy touched the back of his hand. "This level of anxiety is out of character for you, my man."

He grinned, took a sip of coffee, then slumped back in the seat, resting against its low back. "I know. Honestly, I almost didn't have her come out here. And I changed my mind a couple of times even after I made the arrangements. I've been driving Henry crazy about it."

Something spiked in Quincy's gut. Jack and Henry were two of her best friends. They'd even moved to the island with her, completely abandoning their life in L.A. "Why are you, or Missy for that matter, so worked up about this?"

"I don't know. She just seemed so concerned, that I

guess it got me worked up, too.

"Jack, I know I don't know your niece like you do. But in my opinion, she's very hard on herself. And please don't take this the wrong way, but she's a capable adult. And no matter what her level of self-confidence may be, I'm pretty sure she's capable of running her own career. I hear this is her second one."

Jack nodded, and a long pause hung between them. "You're not wrong. About any of that."

Wanting to move away from a deep dive into Missy's psyche and prevent any accidental disclosures Quincy might make about her inappropriate observation of the way Missy bit her lip when she was nervous or toyed with her hair when she was unsure, Quincy pivoted to talking about the coming day's activities. But even as she sipped her coffee and strategized with her good friend, Quincy hid the swirling thoughts she'd been having about making Missy her fake bride.

****

Quincy sat on a patch of rough grass. A scruffy terrier mix, Harold, lay across her lap. Harold's parents had failed to mention that he was an extremely anxious little dude. So she'd been unprepared. And when they dropped him off that morning on their way to the opposite side of the island for an extended vacation, Harold had decided that only Quincy could calm the raging fear that lived inside him.

Harold was now attached to Quincy like a strong magnet stuck permanently to the refrigerator. Quincy would need some time to work with Harold enough to get him to trust someone else so Quincy could leave his sight and film the segments for the show. That wasn't going to happen today, and Jack and the film crew didn't have time to coddle a dog. But Quincy always put the dogs first, so it was the show that would have to suffer to accommodate Harold.

As it turned out, the little hang-up gave Missy a chance to shine. She'd been working hard for nearly a month and thrown everything she had into the show. She listened, she never complained, and she was great with the dogs. Sure, some of the dogs recognized her as a softy and took advantage. As a trainer, that was her biggest weakness, but it certainly wasn't the worst possible one.

The longer she stayed, the more she'd also started to come out of her shell. Over the past two weeks, the shyness Quincy had once assumed was natural revealed itself to be much more situational. When Missy was joking around with her uncles or the film crew members she'd befriended, she exuded a confidence that was impossible to miss.

So today, when they realized that Quincy would be hampered by a furry ball of anxiety named Harold, Missy had suggested they film the dog b-roll, something they usually peppered throughout the week. Quincy agreed, suggesting that Missy work with the dogs to help the film crew get close ups of them running, sitting, smiling, and generally being adorable.

Now, as they executed Missy's plan, Quincy and Harold sat in one corner of the training field. Unfortunately, her view wasn't perfect. The cameras and lighting equipment took precedence over her ability to properly observe, but she could see the action well enough to tell that Missy was getting it done. Jack and Jason must have agreed because they kept calling out compliments on the shots they were getting.

There were so many things about Missy that made her

perfect for the show: her easy acceptance of Quincy's rules for handling the dogs and the diligent way she followed them, her quiet nature, her perfectionism that nearly matched Quincy's own. She wasn't so confident with cameras, as was evidenced by the way she kept biting her lip and playing with strands of her hair. But it didn't really matter since she herself wasn't on camera.

Missy could be counted on. And that's why Quincy resurrected the idea she'd first formed after the meeting with Myra at her house a few weeks ago. The one she'd shoved aside when her dreams got too spicy. Missy could help Quincy in more ways than one.

She'd never completely let go of the idea, and this morning's phone call from the mainland had added to the building blocks of a plan. Gina had scored a part in a relatively popular movie, and she was doing the late-night television circuit. She'd mentioned Quincy in an interview last night, dragging her back into the shit show of what Olivia had started calling the "Gina affair."

Not even Quincy's move to the island her mother was born and raised on could stop her from being the center of attention back in L.A. She needed to keep everyone off her back, and with things escalating quickly, she would have to act fast.

That's why the ridiculous idea she'd shoved into the corner of her mind three weeks ago was floating back to the surface. In the light of day, it didn't seem so off the wall. Maybe it was even practical.

When the film crew stopped for the day, Missy stumbled over to Quincy, surrounded by six tired dogs. "Do you want me to take them back to the kennels before I head out for the night?"

"Yeah, sure." Quincy stroked Harold's wiry fur. "If you're not busy, would you like to have dinner with me tonight?"

Missy frowned. Not a great sign. "I feel bad about how much you already cook for me, with lunches and all."

Hopefully the frown was just guilt. That could be overcome. "No. I meant at Stevie's."

Missy's eyes popped. "Stevie's?"

"It's a local favorite." It was perfect. It wasn't too intimate and had just the right mix of casual and platonic that they needed for this kind of conversation.

"Sure. That sounds great."

Quincy rose to her feet.

Missy pointed at Harold. "What about him?"

"We'll get an outside table on the patio. He can sit there with us. Let's get the rest of these babies back to the kennels, and we'll head up there in my car."

Quincy moved along the path with purpose. Now that her mind was made up, there would be no more stalling. She was going to make this deal tonight.

Chapter 3

Make the Deal

Stevie's was Henry's favorite restaurant, so Missy had already been twice. Hidden away from the main drag and disguised with a rusty sign and broken-down exterior, it tended to repel tourists. That feature, along with an interior that could be the dictionary definition of cozy, made it a quintessential local hang-out.

Dark booths with overstuffed seats lined both walls; a narrow walkway between them led from the kitchen to the bar. The bar itself had the iconic look of a classic watering hole. A thick slab of ancient wood topped the surface. On one side, floor to ceiling shelves of liquor were backed by mirrors and stained glass. Opposite that, a set of spindly bar stools invited bottoms to be planted on their worn surfaces.

The patio was a simple rectangle extending out the back. A jumble of wobbly wooden tables and spindly chairs crowded onto uneven brick pavers. With no canopy, the space afforded an unobstructed view of the balmy evening sky, which contrasted against the dark bar.

The patio was a much better place to hang out with her boss, so Missy relaxed a little when they settled into a table near the center of the outdoor space. They got Harold situated on a soft pad Quincy had brought and laid beside her chair. Moments after they sat down, a server appeared with two glasses and a bottle of wine. "The Syrah today?"

Missy did not miss how that looked. "You must be a regular."

"I am. I love this place." Quincy turned to the server. "We'd love the Syrah, Greta." Quincy's gaze skipped over to Missy. "At least I would. Do you like red wine, Missy?"

"Yes. I love it. Uncle Jack is an aficionado. He taught me everything I know about wine."

The server indicated a question with the raised bottle, and Quincy nodded. She thanked the hostess as she finished pouring. Then she raised her glass, and Missy mirrored her. "To your Uncle Jack."

Missy knew her smile was so big it must have looked comical, but she couldn't help it. She was sitting across from her gorgeous boss after a day at her dream job on a beautiful island. And it had gone so well. She ran the entire show as Quincy watched. The dogs responded to her, and everything had clicked.

"Yes. To Uncle Jack indeed."

They clinked glasses and each took a drink.

"Are you ready to order, or can we just talk for a minute?" Quincy asked.

Missy's stomach swam, and all thoughts of dinner fled. Was this more than it appeared? More than just a casual dinner with the boss? "Whatever you'd like."

"Seems that's always your answer." Quincy tipped her head. "But I want to know about you. Are you starving?"

"No. I'm enjoying this wine, though."

"Great. Let's talk then. Greta will bring bread. If you want to eat after you hear what I have to say, we'll indulge in a great meal. Their veggie lasagna is incredible."

"Okay." Missy's brain shifted into full panic mode. What the hell did that mean? If she wanted to eat after whatever Quincy had to say? What was happening? Was she about to get fired?

Missy tasted blood. She'd bitten a little too hard on her lower lip. She pulled her lip out from between her clenched teeth and licked the spot. Quincy's eyes pinned to her, gaze intent on Missy's mouth.

"Hey," Quincy said. "Don't be nervous. This isn't a bad conversation. At least I don't think so."

"Can you just tell me what you're talking about, because it's making me really anxious."

Quincy reached across the table and placed her hand over Missy's, fingertips resting lightly over knuckles. "I'm sorry I'm being so cryptic. I don't mean to be. This is just a really strange thing to ask someone, and I guess I'm trying to figure out how to do it."

"Just ask." The suspense was like a vice gripping Missy's chest, and she really needed it to stop.

"Okay. Here goes. Will you marry me?"

This couldn't really be happening. She skipped through all the possibilities. Perhaps she was hallucinating under the influence of a sickness or a substance she didn't remember taking. Perhaps this was some sort of weird practical joke. Or maybe Quincy was high. Or was this like a thing for the show? Were there hidden cameras on her right now? She swiveled her head, peering toward the corners of the tiny patio, but saw nothing.

As if to punctuate her confusion, Harold let out a grumble and stretched out across the mat beside Quincy's chair. Quincy patted his side then returned her attention to Missy. "Here's the thing, that conversation with Myra about my ex—as much as I hate to say it, Myra's right about one thing. Getting married would solve this problem for me, quell the talk, get Gina off my back."

"Uh huh." Missy swallowed hard. To combat the dry

taste in her mouth, she took a long sip of her wine. She eyed the bottle sitting at the center of the table, grateful Greta had left it behind.

Quincy cleared her throat. "Gina and I had a long-term relationship back in L.A. We were together during the rise for both of us. I established my training business and landed the show. She got a lead role in a television series. We were building our careers. We were young, successful, and we kind of became an "it" couple for the queers. You know, fame, lights, camera, cute dogs. But it went wrong. We weren't right for each other anymore. We grew apart. I don't know, I guess I could say a million things about that, but what I'll say is that it turned bad like milk forgotten in your trunk. And I left her. And she got possessive. And that made me very uncomfortable. So I picked up my whole life, my business, my show, everything, and I moved to this island to live on my family's property and resume my career far away from her."

Quincy leaned back and took a sip of her wine as Greta returned with a wicker basket stuffed with bread and tiny ceramic ramekins overflowing with flavored butters. Quincy smiled and thanked Greta, her voice smooth, like she had no cares in the world.

Meanwhile, Missy was completely incapable of speech.

When they were alone again, Quincy ran her hand over her face, her palm coming to rest on her neck. "I don't regret the move for a second. It changed my whole life. My training business and the show were doing okay in L.A., but both are really thriving here."

Quincy leaned forward, placing her half empty wine glass on the table. Missy picked up the bottle and refilled Quincy's glass as well as topping off her own. This conversation was unimaginable. Wine would surely help.

"And I'm not interested in dating right now. I want to focus on the business, the show, and the dogs. So, I've been thinking about it a lot, and I think that a good, solid solution to my troubles may be to be off the market altogether."

"So you want to get married?"

Quincy tipped her head. "Is that ridiculous?"

How could she possibly respond to that? It was bizarre, unexpected, shocking even. "Ridiculous isn't the word I would use."

Quincy laughed. "How about a little extreme?"

"That's better." It did seem like a lot, but the motivation for Quincy wanting to get married was secondary to the bigger question looming in Missy's mind. She couldn't find a tactful way to ask it. Instead, it poured out of her like the wine from the bottle. "Why me? What makes me a good choice for your marriage of convenience?"

Even as she was adjusting to the idea of Quincy choosing this bizarre route to freedom from her ex, she couldn't help but imagine Quincy with all manner of glamorous people. If she didn't want someone with notoriety, and instead was looking to marry an employee, Gabriela, who was about as graceful and lovely a person as Missy had ever seen, was a much better candidate than her.

"Well, that's the thing." Quincy became more animated, her eyes brighter, her shoulders higher. "You and I work together, but I don't pay you. I am not technically your employer. And we get along well."

It was as if Quincy had read her mind; which made her wonder, had Quincy already considered and rejected Gabriela because she was employed directly by Quincy in her dog training business? A tinge of pain struck her chest.

"I see." The words came out of her with surprising calm.

"We work in the same business and understand what that takes and what it means. We both prefer animals to people. And, for now, we are both living on an island in the Caribbean away from most of our friends and family, your uncles excluded, of course. If two people are going to do something like this, those factors all seem like they'd help."

Missy nearly choked as that last sentence dredged up something inside her. Her personal history with notoriety was an old wound that had never truly healed. Even taking this job had been a concern for her. But Jack had promised that she'd go under the radar of any press the show received. He'd even left her name off the credits. Now Quincy was talking about a marriage that would be announced on social media in a big splashy way.

"Will the island really protect us?"

"From what?"

"You know." Missy waved her hand in the air. "Like being on the gossip shows, podcasts, et cetera."

Quincy pursued her lips and squinted her eyes for a moment. "In a way. I mean, it's not like L.A. Reporters would be stationed outside my house. If that's what you mean."

"But would they talk about us, L.A. reporters?"

"Is that a problem?"

How could she possibly explain? She had nothing to hide. No skeletons were rattling around in her closet, just the trauma of a queer teenager who'd been used as a publicity weapon by unscrupulous media whores. She was an adult now and hadn't been in the news in years. It hardly seemed something that would exceed Quincy's need to get out from under a toxic ex.

Was she actually thinking about doing this? Fuck. She was. But if the press was a concern she didn't want to voice, there were still others she could ask about. "What about living arrangements?"

Quincy let out a breath. "So, you're considering it?"

"I guess so. But I have more questions."

Quincy took a sip of wine and looked at Missy over the rim of her glass. "I was thinking we could share the house. It's not huge, but big enough for two. The spare room is practically empty, so there would be plenty of room for your stuff. And we already work together. I think all of that would be rather easy. Don't you?"

Missy swallowed hard as she ruminated on the idea of seeing Quincy first thing in the morning, wearing nothing but a tank top and boy shorts. She wasn't used to having crushes, and her quickly growing infatuation for Quincy presented unfamiliar problems, especially in a scenario where they would be sharing a home. "Yeah. For sure."

"I do have one concern, though."

Only one? Missy had so many concerns her head spun. "What's that?"

"What about your family? How would that work?"

Apparently, Quincy had considered how this would affect Missy, at least marginally. "Well, we'd have to tell Jack and Henry the whole story, obviously. I think I could talk them into telling the rest of my family that it's all, you know, real. Truth be told, if we told them all it was just a..." Missy waved her hand in the air, searching for the right word.

"Business deal?"

"Yeah. That might work, too. They're very business-minded people."

"They do have that reputation."

Missy wasn't surprised that Quincy had heard about her family, not just from Jack, but in general. They owned a company that was a San Francisco icon and weren't exactly hidden from the public eye.

"What would you tell your family?"

"As little as possible." Quincy didn't elaborate on that statement. Instead, she grabbed a roll and started buttering it. "So, you want to have dinner?"

Despite the sensations swimming around in her gut, Missy nodded. "I want to try that veggie lasagna."

Quincy raised her wine glass, flashed Missy a smile that could melt a glacier, and said, "Lasagna it is."

****

When Missy was thirteen, her brother, Matt, fell in love with a woman named Elaina. She'd snagged Matt's complete loyalty and devotion, and it didn't take long before Elaina was Missy's sister-in-law. She was the coolest person alive, and she treated Missy like a favorite protégé.

She was also brutally honest about absolutely everything. Which was why it was a complete mystery to Missy why she repeatedly chose Elaina as a confessor. Elaina claimed that the reason Missy told her everything was that she wanted to hear the complete, unfiltered truth, something everyone else in her family had always coddled her too much to actually give her. Whatever the deal really was, Missy was on the phone with Elaina, once again spilling her guts.

"Okay. Back up," Elaina said. "She just randomly asked you to marry her?"

Missy sighed. She'd already told the whole story. Why

didn't Elaina just digest it and give her some advice? "I mean, it wasn't random. And she said she's been thinking about it for weeks."

"That's interesting. I wonder what's been going on in her mind?"

Missy did, too. But their speculation wasn't going anywhere. "Come on, Elaina. Tell me what to do."

"It sounds like you already said yes, so what do you want from me?"

Missy's chest squeezed. It wasn't the marrying Quincy part that ramped up her anxiety. It was the telling her family part. Elaina was right. It was a done deal. Now she had to take the next steps. There was no delaying it. No stopping it.

"You're right."

"Are you regretting your decision?"

Was she? She imagined sitting across the kitchen island from Quincy in the morning, a mug of coffee perched in front of each of them, Quincy's face soft with sleep. No regrets to be found there.

"No. I would just like to do it without telling anyone."

Elaina laughed. "I felt pretty much the same way when your brother proposed. You think your family is a lot? You've met mine, right?"

"And after it was over?"

"It was fine. But I have to tell you, Missy. My marriage was real. This might not land the same way."

And that was the needle in her side, the prick in her heart. Over the course of her sleepless night, she'd come to realize that in her heart she wanted to do this. Despite running over that desire a million times in her head, wringing it through a pros and cons list and every other decision-making tool she'd ever heard about, she couldn't name why. But she also couldn't deny that it was there.

So she'd made up her mind. But would her decision hurt her family? Would it hurt her?

"How does it land with you?"

Elaina's heavy breath hit the phone. "I'm not sure. I mean, my concern is you. I don't know Quincy. Her needs are not on my radar. You are who I care about. So, my question is: What are you getting out of it?"

Missy had no idea how to answer that question. Her motivation for agreeing was tenuous, sketchy, and all caught up in fangirl admiration as well as a completely new situation. As a demisexual, she'd never had a crush on someone she didn't know well, and she had no idea where to go with the sensations Quincy stirred in her.

But that particular piece of her identity provided an answer to Elaina's question. "I think you know that I haven't had a lot of good luck with relationships."

"I know, Missy. But you're young, and you haven't had that many tries."

"Hear me out. I'm here on an island with, like, 40,000 people. So the odds of me finding the right person are even slimmer than they were in San Francisco. And someone I admire has asked for my help. I'm in a position to help her. It just feels right to me."

A long pause followed her statement. She chewed her lip as she waited for Elaina's response.

"What about your money?"

Missy couldn't help but chuckle. "Do you think Quincy is a gold digger? You should see the property she lives on."

"I don't know her. I know she's a friend of Jack's, so sure, it's far-fetched that she's marrying you for your money. I'm just looking out for you here, Missy. You have a very big trust fund, and you're talking about entering a marriage without love."

"We're going to do a prenup. And I told you, this is about helping Quincy out of a bind. We'll get a divorce after a bit, and we'll both be the same as we were before."

"What about the press?"

The shaky feeling that first filled her on consideration of Quincy's proposal flooded over her again. She'd avoided this particular issue during her ruminations last night. "We think it won't be so bad. Especially with us being isolated on this island."

Elaina made a sound low in her throat. "Okay. I got your back. Text me after you tell everyone, and I will run interference."

"I love you so much."

"I love you, too. I hope this isn't a huge fuck up."

****

Uncle Jack slowly ran his fingertip over the space above his upper lip as his gaze shifted from Missy to Quincy and back again. He perched tenuously in the patio chair and squinted his eyes against the sun.

Uncle Henry, on the other hand, was not at a loss for words. "The logistics aren't what concerns me." He'd managed to sit quietly through the long explanation of why they were getting married as well as all the practical things like living arrangements and prenuptial agreements. "I want to talk about you." He pointed to Missy. "Your life, your future, and how this will affect it."

Missy turned to Quincy, who'd sat beside her through all of it, contributing and talking openly and honestly with her uncles. But now Quincy leaned back and stared at Missy. "Quincy?" she asked, hoping for some help. Though she didn't know why she thought Quincy could answer Henry's questions. None of those things seemed to be included in Quincy's plans.

Quincy gazed back at her. "The question is for you, Missy. And it's a good one. I don't want to be a negative in your life."

That was something at least. Missy had spent three sleepless nights pondering every aspect of this deal. They'd worked out a million little details together during each day, but it was only at night, when she was alone with her thoughts and feelings, that Missy really considered what it all meant.

This marriage wasn't designed to last. The deal wasn't defined by a specific set of dates, but they agreed that it would only be viable as long as it was practical and fulfilled the necessary needs it was created to manage. Quincy's needs.

Snagging a chance to get what she wanted, Missy finally exposed her own motivations. "I'll be honest. I need to make my own way. I'm twenty-six, and I have been living in the shadow of my family name for every one of those years. I even got this job because of you." She gestured to Jack before dropping her hands on her thighs.

She hadn't planned this rant, but now that it was happening, she embraced it. The thought had been just forming when she talked to Elaina on the phone the other day, and now it popped into her head with greater ferocity.

"I could be the most brilliant dog trainer ever, but it will still be Missy Green, heir to the famous San Francisco family fortune. Missy Green, playing at dog training. I can change that by changing the source of my notoriety. Alter the dynamics. I don't know if it will work. But it could give me a chance to try to shine for who I am. Maybe Quincy can help me do that."

Quincy nodded. "I don't know if it will work either. But I'm willing to do everything I can to help you make a name for yourself."

Missy turned to Quincy, a new idea blossoming in her head at that very moment, begging to get out. "Let me take your last name."

Missy wasn't certain what to expect from that request, but Quincy just casually lifted one shoulder. "Sure."

Uncle Jack's frown when she so easily abandoned the family name wasn't surprising. But that wasn't what he addressed. "Okay. Let me be more specific about my concern. What about your personal life? What if you fall in love with someone else?" He pointed at Missy making it clear that his concern was for her, not Quincy.

Quincy dropped her hand to the table. "Then we divorce. No problem."

"Or," Jack said, "you could just say you're married. Not legally do this at all."

Missy couldn't stop the guffaw that came out of her mouth. "Uncle Jack, can you imagine the social-media scandal that would result if we got found out."

"I'm with Missy on that," Henry said. "If they're going to do it, they have to actually do it. There is something else though." He moved his fingers between them. "This is an age-gap romance, sweeties."

Missy rolled her eyes. "Since when does anybody care about that? Besides, I think that's a bit of an exaggeration."

Quincy made a sound, gathering Missy's attention. She raised an eyebrow. "You said twenty-six, right?"

Missy nodded.

Quincy shrugged. "I'll be forty next year."

"Whatever, not even fifteen years." Missy dismissed

the issue with a wave of her hand.

"What about money?" Jack leaned forward, elbows on the wrought iron table. "I don't mean to be a dick, but I don't want to see this get messy, Q." He stared right at Quincy.

Missy bristled. "Uncle Jack. I'm not a child."

"No," Quincy said. "You're not. But you do have a massive trust fund, and your uncle wants to make sure it's safe."

Missy was used to her family talking about her like she was incapable of taking care of herself. The consummate baby of the family. She hated it, but it wasn't a surprise. Having Quincy participate, however, was a punch to the gut.

"It's not so much that," Uncle Jack said. "It's just that emotions and money don't mix well. Getting married with no emotions looks simple, but things happen."

"Here." Missy shoved a folder, containing a prenup between her and Quincy, at her uncle. When Quincy had suggested that they bring it along, Missy had protested. She didn't think it was any of her uncles' business what paperwork they chose to sign. They were two consenting adults. But now her anger was overwhelming her, and she was using it to fuel her moves. "Take a look."

Jack slowly leafed through the folder, making a bunch of humming noises before passing it over to Henry and looking at Quincy with a grin. "It's perfect. Every 'i' dotted. Every 't' crossed."

"Did you expect anything less from me?" Quincy said.

Everything about the exchange, from their words to the way Jack and Quincy looked at each other as peers, made Missy feel young and childish. But worse, she felt like a commodity. A walking, talking bride to be purchased, the exchange to be handled by the adults. The sensation itched on her skin, hindering her ability to sit still.

She rose. “Stop. I am making this choice. It’s mine to make. You.” She pointed at Jack. “Don’t get a say. Nor do you.” She shifted the end of her weaponized finger toward Henry. “We came here to tell you as a courtesy and to ask if you wanted to participate. We didn’t come here for permission. And you.” She turned toward Quincy and dropped her fists onto her hips. Her resolve almost faltered as she stared down the smooth, regal face. “You aren’t negotiating with them. You are making this deal with me.”

While all three sat there with mouths agape, Missy decided to hold onto the power surging through her. “This conversation is over, and I'm walking back to Quincy’s. Goodnight.” Then she turned on her heel and left.

Chapter 4

Remember to Remain Professional

The officiant was stunning in a long black dress and heels. Quincy would have been reeling if the woman she was marrying weren't even hotter in a sexy mint green cocktail dress and strappy sandals, dark hair piled on top of her head in a riot of rich spiraling curls.

Quincy had never spent much time imagining her wedding. She'd been with Linda Ackerman back when Obergefell was decided at the Supreme Court and gay marriage was legalized across the country. They'd discussed tying the knot while standing hand-in-hand at a pro-marriage equality rally. Even in that emotional moment, she still didn't have a clear picture in her mind of what it would look like, where it would be, or what she'd be wearing.

But she'd woken up that morning with the desire to look good for Missy. She'd chosen a sharp, light gray suit with her favorite rainbow-colored tie. She'd managed to wrangle her hair into a much slicker version of the usual easy, cropped style she wore daily.

She was glad she'd gotten the bug because Missy had turned up at the beach looking like a runway model. The graceful woman she was about to marry was so stunning the air caught in her throat, making it hard for Quincy to breathe. She tugged at her tie and tried to count her breaths, three seconds inhale, three seconds exhale.

Jack and Henry were both dressed for the occasion, too. They wore smiles despite the discontent Quincy knew they felt over the entire situation. The image of Missy standing her ground in front of her uncles demanding that they give her agency over her own life flashed through Quincy's head. Missy was fierce and demanding, and so utterly gorgeous in that moment that Quincy wouldn't have denied her anything. So when they got home, and Missy asked that they elope on the beach, Quincy made it happen.

And here they were.

Missy walked toward her, an uncle on either side; Quincy instinctively straightened her shoulders. Missy arrived, and Jack and Henry peeled off to stand a few feet away in the soft sand. They were the only witnesses to this event, aside from Myra and the thousands of people who would later watch the video she was taking on social media.

"Ready?" Joy, the officiant, asked.

Quincy looked over at Missy, who nodded confidently. That was good enough for her. "Yes. We're ready."

"Great. Let's get started." Joy proceeded to give a brief speech about what marriage meant.

Quincy had completely overlooked this bit in all her planning and scheming. And now she stood here steeped in these words, in this tradition, in the meanings it conjured. This ritual was so hard won for the queer community. And she was taking it for granted.

Each word penetrated her like a knife. She was willfully violating an institution she and many others had fought hard to make available to everyone. The moment Kris Perry and Sandy Stier said "I do" in front of Kamala Harris in the San Francisco City Hall was a monument she was defacing by engaging in a fake marriage.

But something shifted inside her, overtaking the dark cloud of guilt, when they recited the vows. She stood there, mouthing the words as she repeated after Joy. What was she really saying? She promised to love, honor, and cherish a beautiful, talented woman. And fake marriage or not, Quincy thought she could live up to most of that, even if only for a short time.

When she slid the plain platinum ring on Missy's finger, guilt fled entirely and excitement built in her chest. She was taking the plunge, doing the very thing she'd held signs about in the burning sunlight of a Sacramento summer. She was currently enacting the thing she shouted about until she was hoarse in front of City Hall, the very right she'd ridden a bus across the country to DC to stand on the steps of the Supreme Court for. She'd been there when they announced the decision that changed so many lives and made this exact moment possible.

Something else struck her when Missy slipped an identical ring on her own finger, but it was wispy and undefined, a formless sensation that could not be pinned down. Quincy let it roll over her, straightened her shoulders, and moved on. She waited for the moment that would signal the end of the ritual—when the officiant announced them spouses for life.

But she'd forgotten a step. That one little piece that seemed inconsequential before now loomed over them as Joy told them to kiss, sealing the deal. She'd completely overlooked this part, and now it swallowed her up in expectation.

Quincy leaned forward to plant a short and sweet peck on her bride. But as soon as their lips met, the world tilted. Quincy's body acted without conscious thought. Her arm wrapped around Missy's waist, pulling her body flush against Quincy. When Missy's mouth opened,

Quincy had no choice but to take advantage, if only for a moment.

What should have been brief and blunt became something else—something sensual and intense. Quincy pulled away in shock. An electrical current blazed through her. She glanced at her bride, searching for an answer, recognition, something. Had Missy felt that, too? But she'd never know, because Missy had already turned away and was hurrying toward her uncles, the divots in the sand where she'd stood left in her wake, just like that kiss.

****

Quincy held the door for Jack as he ambled in with two matching suitcases, one in each hand. Missy slid in quietly behind him, a large handbag slung over one shoulder and a leather computer case over the other. Once they were past her, Quincy peered out at the driveway. Henry waved from the front seat of the still running car.

A filling dinner at Stevie's had followed the ceremony, something Henry and Jack insisted on. A celebration was always in order when a gay wedding happened, Jack said.

After dinner, Henry and Jack had taken Missy away with the promise to return her and her things before bedtime. And here she was, with all the belongings she'd been able to squeeze onto the plane from San Francisco.

Quincy was still standing at the door when Jack and Missy emerged from the spare bedroom. They stopped a few feet from her, and Jack turned to his niece. "Remember you promised you'd come over tomorrow morning, and we'll call your parents from our place."

"I'm not going to break my promise, Uncle Jack. We'll be there." Missy's gaze touched Quincy.

"We'll be there." Stiffness inhabited every part of Quincy and seemed to echo in her voice. She rolled her shoulders in a failed attempt to relax.

"Besides," Missy said. "Uncle Henry promised us quiche."

Jack—her friend, her producer, her peer—stared at Quincy for a long moment, a million unsaid things rolling in the air between them. Then he nodded and left.

Quincy closed the heavy front door and moved into the living room. Missy hovered near the couch, her fingers intertwined, her calf muscles pumping as she pressed up onto her toes, dropped down, then pressed up again.

"Do you want a drink?" Quincy asked.

"God, yes."

"Sit down. I'll bring you one of my famous margaritas."

Missy moved over to the sectional and perched delicately on one end. "Sounds great. I love margaritas."

Quincy turned to the small wet bar that sat at one end of the room. She'd considered removing it when she first bought the house, but had since come to appreciate it. On the rare occasions she had someone over, it allowed her to make drinks for her guests and still engage in casual conversation.

A person could never ask something too intense when the host was fixing them a drink. They had to concentrate. So, the act lent itself to small talk. Also, with the wet bar, guests didn't get an opportunity to think up a deeply personal question to ask like they could in the deep silence that accompanied a host's absence to another room to prepare beverages. The wet bar provided the perfect solution to all that hosting awkwardness, and so she'd ultimately decided to keep it. And she was glad she had because now, it allowed her to bring up completely innocuous questions with her new bride.

"What are your favorite drinks?"

"I like whatever. I haven't found anything I don't like yet. Random question: Why don't you have a dog of your own?"

"That is a great question." This was a topic Quincy could handle. Before answering, she paused to shake the drinks. When she was done, she poured them into two glasses and walked over to Missy, handing her a glass filled to the brim with light green liquid.

"I've never had a dog that was mine." Quincy suppressed a chuckle at the shocked expression on Missy's face. "Strange, huh?"

"No offense, but yeah."

Quincy settled on the opposite end of the couch, leaving a gap of at least two and half feet between them. "Growing up, my parents and brothers always had a dog that was like their dog, right? So, we always had at least four dogs at any given time, but they were all claimed by someone else. I could have asked for my own dog. But I never did, because I was always too busy training their dogs. They were terrible about it. They would get a dog and then do nothing with it, no attention, no training. Sometimes they didn't even remember to feed them. So, I took the role of caretaker and trainer for all their dogs. When someone's dog would pass, they would immediately go to the shelter and bring home a new one. And I'd take care of it too."

"So, in a way you had lots of dogs."

"In a way, I did. But I never got to pick the dog out from the shelter or name it." She shrugged. "Anyway. After I left home, I didn't get a dog of my own because I had this stupid idea." Quincy ran a hand over her hair. Was she really about to admit this to someone? And why had she chosen her new, fake bride to do it with? She could stop this train altogether and refuse to answer. But she honestly didn't want to, and Missy's adorable face, filled with curiosity, was irresistible as she waited for an answer.

"What was the idea?"

"I wanted to pick out a dog with someone—you know, someone special. And my first serious girlfriend was allergic. My last ex, Gina, hated dogs."

"Wait. How did you end up dating someone who hates dogs?"

Now they were in seriously dangerous territory. How and why she was with Gina in the first place was, in many ways, still a mystery to her. Quincy had no choice but to change the subject. "It's a long story. What about you? You've had dogs, I assume?"

"The love of my life died last year. She was a pittie mix I rescued when she was just a couple of weeks old, dumped by someone in a garbage can. Her name was Jenna. She was with me for thirteen years. I didn't feel ready to get another dog." Missy shook her head, and with it seemed to shake off the melancholy that inevitably wrapped around a person when talking about the death of a beloved pet. "It's a good thing, too. It would have been hard to keep up with a puppy, move here, start a new job, and get married." She grinned at Quincy.

That sweet, sassy, little grin caused a wave of some unnamed emotion to roll through Quincy. She took a long sip of her margarita and pressed her hip against the arm of the couch, trying to create even more space between herself and her new bride. "Well, I guess we have lots of dogs now."

Missy laughed, throwing her head back to reveal a smooth, sleek neck; such soft skin would surely feel like silk against Quincy's lips. "Two dozen dogs. Good thing you have a whole team to take care of them all."

Quincy cleared her throat and took another sip of her drink. "The twenty-four we have right now is full capacity, but it isn't always so many. Or at least it didn't used to be."

"I suppose the show has brought you a lot more clients."

"Finding clients for the board and train business was a bit of a struggle at first. Which I didn't expect because the U.S. Virgin Islands don't have a quarantine rule, making it an easy place to bring your dog along compared other tropical location spots. But I had to convince the hotels to recommend me to their guests. We tried billboards on the island and ads in travel magazines. I was desperate to get the business up and running since I'd moved the show here, and I needed the clients to keep that going. It was very much a double stress situation. Though Jack never panicked. His attitude was that if there were only two dogs, we'd still do the show with two dogs. But the boarding and training business did take off, and that helped the show, which is now doing better than ever." She shrugged to disguise her pride. "So not bad for a sudden and unexpected move to the middle of the Caribbean, I guess."

There were a million more things to say about that move: Gina, her parents, the need to claim a part of her life and heritage for herself. But unlike the relatively innocuous overshare about her desire to co-parent a dog, these items lay in a vault she never opened to anyone, and she wasn't about to start with her temporary wife.

Instead, she stayed silent as Missy took a sip of her drink; her eyes pinned to a tiny drop of liquid that slipped and landed on the spot just below the little bow of her lower lip. Her pink tongue darted out and scooped it up. Quincy's heart pounded in her chest.

"I'm lucky, too," Missy said. "To get this gig. To get this opportunity to learn from you."

"You might say that now. But once Myra sends out the pictures of our wedding, things could get intense."

Missy shrugged, but her shoulders were stiff. "I'm used to it."

Quincy wondered about her life. Missy had said she wanted to change her name. There had to be a story there. "I guess you probably are. But I'm not. I didn't really understand what I was getting into when I agreed to do this show. I was just a dog trainer in L.A. who happened to score a couple of famous clients. One day, one of them introduced me to Killian Rogue. The next thing I know, he's funding the show and Jack is putting me on camera. It was like that." She snapped her fingers. "I suppose that sounds stupid."

Missy placed her drink on the coffee table and leaned toward Quincy. "No. It doesn't sound stupid at all." She reached over and placed her hand over Quincy's. "Every one of my friends, everyone I've ever dated, they're all in the same boat. They got unexpected attention and didn't know how to deal with it."

Quincy wanted the story desperately now, but she wasn't entirely sure how to pry it out of Missy. "Because they were with you?"

"Yeah. My family name is very visible where I grew up. I was the youngest in the family, and the only girl. There were pictures of me in the paper on the day I was born. And almost every year when I was kid there would be some story in the San Francisco Chronicle about the family when my parents made a big donation to a charity, or when my grandparents each died, or when their business had a round of layoffs. And every time the press would pull up my school picture or a family picture with me in it, or something. Most of my family didn't mind the attention. But I never got used to it. When I was a teenager, it got worse. If I ended up at a party, someone inevitably put a picture of me taking a shot on social media. And when I came out as queer, I knew it would blow up in all the wrong ways. My whole family thought it wouldn't be too bad for me since Uncle Jack already had been out for decades at that point. But there were still issues." Missy had been steaming through the story, and she suddenly stopped, her gaze moving to her hands, which were now both back in her lap.

"But now you're here, on an island, married to me."

Missy looked up at Quincy from under long lashes. "Yeah. They quit bugging me by sophomore year in college, to be honest. But I never really got over it, you know?"

"And now you'll be in the public eye again."

Missy shrugged. "Somehow it feels different."

Quincy opened her mouth to ask Missy exactly how it would be different, but before she could get the words out, Missy asked, "You grew up in L.A., right?"

Quincy fell back into the couch cushions. She might avoid talking about her family, but she could easily regale Missy with the sights and sounds of L.A. They spent the next hour talking over the similarities and differences of growing up in Southern versus Northern California.

More than once, Quincy found herself laughing. Missy was an excellent storyteller. The way she wove the tale of how she and her best friend in high school took off during a class trip to Alcatraz and missed their boat, or when Uncle Jack took her to her first drag show in the Castro, kept Quincy following her every word.

Eventually though, Missy yawned. It had been a long day. And Sunday wouldn't bring any rest. They had brunch with Jack and Henry, and they had to make the dreaded phone call to Missy's family. Quincy's shoulders tensed at the thought.

Missy stood, her glass in her hand. "I'll, uh, just wash this."

Quincy reached for the glass. "No, of course not. I'll do it."

Missy moved the glass away from Quincy's fingers. "I live here now, you know."

"Yeah, right. Yeah. Of course."

Missy held out her hand to Quincy. "I'll take yours, too."

She handed her own glass over, fingers brushing Missy's as they slid together over the slick glass.

Missy flashed her an awkward smile. "Okay. Well, I'll just do these dishes real quick and then head to bed."

"Yeah. I'm just gonna go myself then. To bed. So, good night."

Quincy's words made it sound like she was moving toward her stated goal. But for some reason, her feet stayed planted to the plush carpet. Missy stared at her for a moment longer before spinning around and heading to the kitchen at a quick clip.

Quincy let out a breath. This was not going to be easy.

Chapter 5

It's Important to be on the Same Page

Missy rolled her eyes so hard she thought she might sprain her brain. Her mother's voice sprang out of the phone's speaker like a circus announcer on amphetamines. "What do you mean you got married? How could you get married without me there? Jack! How could you let this happen? Henry! Where the hell were you? What is going on?"

"Claire, just calm down a minute," Jack said. "Is Tom there with you?"

Her father's voice glided through the phone in the same deep bass that read Missy bedtime stories when she was a kid. "I'm here, Jack. Why don't you start from the beginning? Claire, sit down and drink this."

Missy could imagine her father ushering her mother into one of the many stately armchairs in their house and handing her a cup of steaming tea. "Mom, Dad. I'm the one who got married, and I'm the one who's going to explain."

Missy glanced at Quincy, who simply nodded. On the walk over this morning, as the bright sun beat down on her shoulders, Missy confessed to Quincy that she didn't want to lie to her family about the real reasons behind their marriage.

"Quincy and I made the decision together to enter a marriage of convenience. It's a business decision for us both."

The long beat that followed Missy's statement felt like a win, until her mother screeched through the phone. "Really, Jack? I didn't realize that by sending my daughter to you, I'd be selling her off to the highest bidder!"

Missy's blood pressure rose. Since when did her mother "send" her anywhere? She wasn't a sixth grader going off to camp. Whether her family acknowledged it or not, she was an adult who made her own decisions.

She wished she hadn't agreed to make this call from her uncles' house. At the time, it seemed like a good way to keep everyone calm. She figured Jack and Henry would be good back-ups against the inevitable backlash. Instead, they were ignoring her agency, and making her look like a child in front of Quincy.

"Claire. Don't be ridiculous," Jack said. "This is a win-win situation. We're all going into it with eyes wide open."

Missy glared at her uncle. "What do you mean, we? We aren't going into anything. I am. I married Quincy. It was my decision. And it's my life."

Her father's soothing tone traveled through the line from the mainland like he was there beside her. "Missy, honey, calm down."

As they always did, those words tugged at the proverbial tail of her already ballooning anger. Throwing a temper tantrum in front of her family wouldn't help her case, but she cared less about that than what Quincy would think of her.

She glanced at Quincy, not at all prepared for what she might see in those striking hazel eyes. Compassion, raw and naked, reflected back at her.

Turning to Missy, Quincy touched her wrist lightly

with the tips of her fingers. "What do you want to do right now, Missy? Go home? Have this conversation another day? I'm following your lead."

Her family loved her; there was no doubt about that. She'd been given everything in life. She was deeply blessed. But she hated the way they thought of her as being under their protection. They didn't see it this way, but to her it was tantamount to being under their control.

Instead of trying to figure out how she wanted to deal with her family at that moment, Missy's mind flashed to the kiss at the wedding ceremony yesterday. First kisses had always been a disappointment. She didn't fully understand why until recently. Digging into demisexuality had shed so much light on the way her sexual feelings were always slow to blossom in comparison to her friends. They would swoon over a man or woman at first sight then talk about first kisses as if they were the end of a long road of deep desire. Missy could never relate.

Usually, her partner kissed her first. They were the ones with the deep desire to taste her. It was the hundredth kiss that really revved her engine, when she was emotionally all-in and then pressed her lips to her partner's catalyzed by all the magical sensations that came wrapped up with her feelings. By then though, the partner was usually getting bored with her.

The kiss yesterday had been different. Fingers of sensation shot up through her chest when Quincy pulled her close. It was so unexpected that Missy had quickly turned away, afraid to look Quincy in the eye.

Now she wanted to chase that sensation, right now, in the middle of this muddled family mess. She twisted her hand around, gripping Quincy's palm and interlacing their fingers. She stood up, pulling Quincy with her. They were facing each other, just as they had been yesterday after the ceremony. She pulled Quincy toward her the way Quincy had done to her.

For the tiniest part of a second, Missy took the time to appreciate how well she and Quincy fit together. Her boney hips snuggled perfectly inside Quincy's wider ones. Her thigh tucked between Quincy's larger ones with the most delicious friction. The swell of Quincy's breasts hit her chest just above her own small ones. Her lips were at Quincy's chin level.

Her smaller stature nearly unraveled her impetuous plan. But, once again, Quincy helped her out. Somehow, she must have understood that all Missy wanted was Quincy's lips on her, and she obliged.

For the space of that kiss, Missy was able to shed everything around her. The overbearing parents on the phone. The loving uncles just feet away on the sun-bleached deck. The fake marriage. The potential for the press to burst back into her life because of it. It was all gone.

All that existed was Quincy's soft lips and the sensation of them moving against hers, Quincy's body smashed against her own, and the absolutely perfect scent that drifted off Quincy—an intoxicating combination of oatmeal soap, fresh flowers, and dog fur. Missy just barely suppressed a groan.

Quincy released her carefully and flashed a small smile before sitting down again. But she kept Missy's right hand, and Missy followed her down, planting herself in her own chair.

"Are you still there, Jack?" Her mother's voice broke through her trance.

"Yeah, we're here. Just watching the newlyweds tongue-wrestle," Jack said.

Technically, there had been no tongue. Though now

that the suggestion was out there, Missy couldn't shove it out of her thoughts. What would that be like?

"What?" Her father sounded so alarmed Missy let out a small chuckle.

"They're kissing, Tom." Henry's deadpan was perfect for the moment.

"I thought it was a fake marriage?"

Henry just laughed.

Missy had no answer for why she'd been compelled to kiss Quincy. But she knew she wanted some time alone to think about it. "We're going home now. I'm not interested in anyone's opinion of my marriage. I'm married. And that's that."

"But Missy—" Her mother started to object.

"Mom. I love you. I will call you later in the week."

Missy didn't wait for a response as she led Quincy out toward the street. Quincy didn't argue. Instead, she matched Missy's steps as they marched away from her family together.

****

"I'm sorry about my family," Missy said as they climbed the small hill toward Quincy's house. She almost said she was sorry for the impromptu kiss as well. But that would be a lie. She wasn't sorry at all for that.

What she was sorry—no, embarrassed about—was her family's reaction to their marriage. Quincy had seen her family's humiliating suffocation act the day they told Jack and Henry about their plans, but this time felt different. She expected her mother to be disappointed that she'd missed the wedding. She knew her father would be confused, and she fully anticipated a little push back when they revealed that the marriage was a business arrangement. But, with the decision already made, the contract signed—literally and figuratively—she'd naively thought things would be different.

Her parents, of course, would be looking out for Missy. That wasn't unexpected. And she had gone into the call knowing they would have her "best interests" at heart. In fact, she'd spent her wedding night tossing and turning in Quincy's spare room thinking through her responses. They ranged from a circuitous and carefully crafted explanation that included her career goals and ideals to a simple "it's my life and I'll do what I want."

Somehow it hadn't come out right, and when the moment of truth came, none of it had come out at all, and Missy had walked away without really explaining herself.

"There's nothing to be sorry for," Quincy said.

Missy wondered if that covered the kiss as well. But she had no idea how to ask that. So instead she said, "My family is kind of a lot."

Quincy chuckled. "Wait 'till you meet mine."

Grateful for the change in subject, Missy seized on it. "What's your family like?"

"Different from yours." The tone of Quincy's voice made it clear that was all Missy would be getting out of her. Then she pivoted the entire conversation. "So, about this honeymoon we promised Myra."

The mention of Myra's social media plans redirected Missy's curiosity. She pulled out her phone to check her socials. Just as she'd promised, Myra had waited until this morning to make any public announcements. The tagged posts had just dropped.

The first thing that caught Missy's eye was a clear image of the marital kiss. The clear image of their faces pressed together and surrounded with muted light was a thing of beauty. It dredged up another round of electricity rippling through Missy. And she wondered again how Quincy felt about that kiss and the one they'd just shared at her uncles' house.

She shoved her phone back into her pocket. "You mean that Myra wants fun honeymoon pictures?"

"Yes, and I think we should take advantage of the opportunity," Quincy said.

A shiver ran through Missy. "What do you mean?"

They crested the hill and the familiar symphony of barking dogs grew louder as they passed near the kennels and play yard. "I mean, I don't know about you, but I could use a break. We can take some pictures for Myra, but I think we should take advantage of the excuse to go on vacation." She stopped to peer over at the beach below them. A streak of morning sunlight hit the sea and bounced up the face of the cliff, highlighting Quincy's features.

Quincy stared toward the water as she continued. "We could get away from all this for a minute." She gestured to the beautiful surroundings. Though Missy knew the beauty wasn't what Quincy meant to get away from. "We could just relax, or have fun, or whatever." She turned to Missy, striking her with clear eyes, filled with an intangible brightness. "What do you think?"

Missy didn't have anything to "get away" from. She loved every day of the life she was living on the island, but the idea of unfettered alone time with Quincy was as desirable as it was terrifying. "I am one hundred percent in."

"Where do you want to go?"

"I'm up for whatever."

Quincy turned toward Missy. "No. Here's the thing. You're going to pick. And whatever you pick, that's what we're going to do."

Missy wasn't entirely certain how to interpret Quincy's motive for wanting her to take the reins on the honeymoon planning. But whatever the reason, she decided not to argue. "Okay. I'll have a full itinerary ready by tomorrow."

****

What would you wear on a honeymoon in a tropical rainforest?

Missy should have known that her text was going to cause the phone to ring, but she'd hoped to avoid an actual conversation. She sighed and answered.

Elaina was worked up. "Seriously. You drop the bomb on your parents days ago and don't respond to any of my texts about it, and then out of nowhere ask me what to wear on your honeymoon? Seriously?"

Missy pulled a pile of underwear and bras out of a laundry basket and dropped them on her bed, instantly wishing she'd had another friend she could ask advice from so she didn't have turn to Elaina. She had Landry here on the island, but they were out on a date with a server from Frankie's, and her relationship with Jason was still too tenuous to approach him in Landry's absence.

"Hey. Sorry. It's just that I'm scrambling to plan a last-minute honeymoon here."

"You need to back so far up."

Missy dropped onto the bed, displacing the pile of lace and silk. She focused on the patterns of sunlight and shadow on the ceiling as she told Elaina every detail of the wedding, the dinner afterward, and the phone call with her parents.

"You left something out."

Missy shifted her gaze to the phone screen as if it was a video call and she could see Elaina's expression, even though she couldn't. "What are you talking about?"

"The wedding night. You skipped from dinner with the uncles to brunch the next morning. There's a great big thing in the middle there."

"No. There isn't. Because it's a fake wedding. Hence, no wedding night. We just talked for a bit and went to sleep. In separate rooms."

"Then what's the point of all this?"

"Elaina. I already told you. Come on."

"Okay. Hear me out. I know you say you don't feel attraction for someone unless you have feelings for them."

"I don't have sexual attraction without feelings, yes, that's correct."

"Right. You aren't attracted to strangers or casual acquaintances or whatever. I know you, and I know that you don't usually reach that gushy, crush-y state until after you're like a month into a relationship. Then, despite the fact that you haven't answered any of my texts where I'm freaking out about what the hell is going on, you send me a random text last night. Let me just read it back to you: Did I mention that my wife has the cutest dimple in her right cheek? It's seriously killing me."

"Shhh. Elaina!" Missy popped her head up to glance at the closed door while her thumb switched the phone off speaker mode.

By the time she had the phone to her ear, Elaina was in full belly laugh. "You're so cute."

"You're a terrible person."

"Since you have the hots for her, you may as well consummate that marriage, you know what I mean?"

"Oh my god. Please stop! I called you about a

honeymoon. Can we just focus for a minute?"

"Girl. You just said honeymoon."

"Okay. Listen. I'm planning the honeymoon, and I need some advice. If I can't get it from you, I will call Jillian."

"You're an asshole."

Missy grinned, knowing that threatening to get advice from Elaina's greatest rival was the best way to get her focused and serious. "You ready to talk turkey now?"

"I hate you. Yeah. Tell me what you got."

Chapter 6

Compromise is Essential

Quincy remained confused about how television "seasons" worked. Growing up, her favorite shows only had one set of episodes per year. When it was over, everyone knew it would be a dry summer filled with reruns until the fall brought a new season.

But things weren't like that anymore. There were some shows with more seasons than their hosts had lived years on the planet. So she just went with the flow. If Jack told her they were done filming a season or ready to start the next one, she marked it in her calendar, checked with her clients, and went with it.

The break between shooting seasons had never meant much to her before. Her business continued to run. The beauty of the island continued to shine into her life. She had a little more time to meet up with friends and acquaintances in town. Occasionally she headed back to the mainland for a quick, obligatory visit, but nothing super exciting.

This time the break meant a two-week honeymoon with her fake bride. As the trip approached, she was both increasingly curious and excited about the plans Missy had kept secret. Surely her anticipation was the result of a deep need for a break from the show and the kennels, but something deep inside nagged at her that more than just a bit of relaxation was the cause.

Quincy stared down at her suitcase, her mind far away from anything resembling a packing list. Instead, it was on kisses. Quincy and Missy hadn't talked about the kiss they shared on their wedding day or the one on the day after; nor had they come close to reenacting them. But Quincy wasn't opposed to the idea, not in the least. They went about their co-habitation like two amenable roommates in St. Croix. Maybe on the honeymoon they could explore a casual, mutually beneficial way to revisit that lip-lock.

Shaking her head, Quincy tried to not to let her thoughts wander in that direction. She needed to stay focused on their professional relationship. Each day on set, Missy proved herself to be hard working and professional. Missy had also shown Quincy a surprising side of herself through the continued negotiations with her parents. With an incredible amount of patience, she called them every few days and re-hashed the same argument over and over again. Quincy mostly left Missy alone to have those conversations in private, but it seemed like Missy was actually making headway.

The slow, torturous progress Missy was determined to make with her family was something Quincy couldn't imagine doing with her own. Sure, she could be endlessly patient with a willful dog; she could sit for hours waiting for the dog to make the right choice for a treat, then do it all over again. But when it came to humans, that was a whole different story. And that was especially true with her brothers and sister-in-law. They were loving, chaotic, and very nosey—a characteristic that only got worse after their parents' death.

If it was Quincy in Missy's shoes, she'd have long since cut off the phone calls and limited their communication to terse texts. Perhaps because her own family knew this, they didn't say a thing during the few calls she'd had with them since the wedding.

She had talked to Olivia about it. For most of her life, Olivia was the only person she ever opened up to. She shared with her best friend things she would never confess to a girlfriend or lover. Gina had suggested, more than once, that if Quincy really wanted a relationship she should get with Olivia. Quincy had just laughed. She couldn't imagine having a relationship with anyone who knew her that well.

It had been nearly three weeks since Myra leaked the news of the wedding. And as much as Quincy avoided social media, Olivia consumed it. According to her, the internet—at least the Queer internet—lost its mind over their nuptials.

Even dog show lovers who weren't at all allies of the queer community were enamored with the whole thing. They waxed philosophical about how Quincy and Missy had bonded over their mutual love of dogs and their matching training techniques. They speculated that perhaps the two had been secretly dating online before Missy even arrived on the island. Quincy personally liked that narrative, even if it was all made up.

With all the online speculation flying around, she was also pretty sure someone in her family had seen all the fuss online about her and Missy tying the knot. But she'd talked to her brother Marc, sister-in-law Keri, and her niece Jordy just a few days ago, and none of them had said a thing. When she spoke to her other brother, Todd, over the weekend, he had rambled on about the goats he was raising on his new property in the valley. In all their talk there was not a single mention of her being suddenly wed.

Quincy stared at the empty suitcase that had jump

started her wandering mind and wondered how one packed for a honeymoon when they had no idea where they were going? Abandoning the suitcase, she meandered out into the main part of the house. She needed to find Missy, but the living room and kitchen were both empty, so she headed down the hall to the guest room. The door stood open, and she peered in.

In her experience, guest rooms tended to be cramped with a small bed and dresser, both previously used by the host and since abandoned. They were usually decorated with every horrible knick-knack and picture gifted to the host by well-meaning friends and family. Or they were a room normally used for working, sewing, or as a kids' playroom that someone haphazardly shoved a bed into.

Quincy, who took a lot of pride in her home and relished finding the most comfortable furnishings for her guests, never understood this seemingly careless approach. People traveled a long way to visit her on this island. So, the guest room here wasn't an afterthought; she needed to provide them with a true reprieve.

This room was well-situated, sitting in a corner of the house which allowed a lot of natural light. It featured a brand-new queen-size bed and a large antique dresser that was lovingly restored by the local antiques guy. Originally, the only way to a bathroom from the guest room was through the hallway. But Quincy had a pocket door installed in the room so that the main bathroom was easily accessible.

While the room was currently empty of life, signs were all around. Both of Missy's suitcases perched on the bed surrounded by piles of clothing. Quincy stepped hesitantly into the room to peer into the luggage. If she could get a glimpse of what Missy was packing, she'd be able to plan her own wardrobe for the trip. The first suitcase was no help. It sat hollow, awaiting its cargo.

The second suitcase contained a riot of silk and lace flowing across the bottom. Delicate, feminine panties and bras tempted Quincy to imagine them on their owner. She shook her head, unwilling to go down that road just now, and went to make her escape. But before she could exit the room, the pocket door to the bathroom opened, and Missy emerged.

Wisps of steam snuck out of the bathroom, clinging to the bare skin of her arms and neck. A handful of wet curls escaped the towel perched on her head. A matching towel barely hid her body from breasts to upper thighs. Missy's legs were not long, but they were exquisitely shaped, like they'd been crafted by a sculptor.

Quincy turned her focus to her breath and hoped that her exterior looked far less chaotic than the roiling thoughts screaming through her brain. Her gaze to lock onto Missy's dark, brown eyes.

"Sorry. So sorry. I was just looking for you." For some reason she pointed her thumb over her shoulder toward the open suitcase with the treasure trove of underwear. She quickly lowered her hand and clasped it with the other one. "I had a question. About packing, actually. That's why I'm here. To ask about packing. But I should come back."

Missy secured her towel with one arm. "No. It's okay. I mean," she glanced down at herself. "My bathing suit is more revealing than this, and you'll see me in that soon enough." A nervous laugh escaped.

Quincy swallowed hard and tried to remember how to move her feet so she could get out of Missy's path to the bed. But she couldn't manage to do it, and as Missy moved, she came close to Quincy, her wet, nearly naked body coming into even better focus.

"What's your question?"

"I have no idea what to pack since I don't know where we're going." She let out a nervous laugh then suppressed a cringe at the sound of it.

"Sorry. I should have said. The weather is very similar to here. No need to pack anything special, except maybe good hiking shoes."

Quincy cocked her head. One of the few things Missy knew about her personally was that Quincy enjoyed trail running. It would have been impossible for her to miss that Quincy left early every morning to run on the steepest, harshest path she could find. In fact, the biggest bonus of her hobby lately was that she'd return from her runs to find a healthy spread of breakfast covering the kitchen island.

"We're going to be hiking?"

"You sound surprised. You think I don't hike?"

Quincy thought she detected a hint of playfulness in Missy's tone. But she was far too tongue-tied to volley Missy's playfulness back. "I guess I don't know."

"Well, I don't run like you. I injured my knee playing soccer in high school. Had to have surgery." Without bending over, Missy pointed toward her right knee. Quincy looked down to see a small scar sitting beside her patella. "Haven't done much running since. But I grew up in the city, walking everywhere, and I love to hike when I'm at parks. My family went to the Sierras a few times a year. Anyway." Missy suddenly stopped talking and glanced down at her suitcase.

Quincy didn't know why, but she took advantage. "Well, good. Thanks for the info. I'll just go finish packing then." She spun on her heel, pushed off the door jamb and plunged through the door.

She practically sprinted down the narrow hall and

looped around when she reached the main room, ducking into the foyer. She hadn't planned a run, she needed to get packed up. But before she could even comprehend what she was doing, her feet were slipping into her running shoes.

She was reaching for her Camelback, knowing it needed a fresh fill of water, when she heard a sound near the kitchen. Unwilling to run into her dripping wet, nearly naked wife again, she abandoned the Camelback, deciding she'd run toward town where she could get water.

She blasted out the back door and started her jog before she'd even left the grassy space behind the house. Focused on running as far away as she possibly could from the desire that shot through her body moments ago, she almost didn't see the ball of wiry fluff barreling toward her from the side.

She barely managed to stop her forward motion before she ran over Harold. He jumped up, his front paws pressing into the flesh just above her knees, and she gave him a generous scratch behind the ear along with a healthy amount of praise for being a good boy. Gabriela appeared, her steps slowing when she saw Harold with Quincy.

"Oh, thank god." She heaved, her hand on her chest as she bent over. "There was a bang." She stuck her thumb over her shoulder. "He took off, and the gate must have been unlatched."

Quincy patted Harold's head. "You don't like those bangs, do you buddy? No you don't, but you gotta stop running away from them. When you go back to the city with your family it will be dangerous if you run into the street."

Her heart clenched at the thought. They'd done a lot

with Harold during his time here. But his family would have to continue to work with him to reinforce and strengthen the training. It would be essential to keeping him safe. Unfortunately, based on the little interaction she'd had with them, she wasn't entirely certain they were up to the task, and it pained Quincy to put his fate in their hands. But that was the job.

"I'll keep working with him until they come." Gabriela approached Harold and clipped a leash on him while he was still distracted by Quincy's ministrations.

Quincy was closing down the board and train for the duration of the honeymoon, allowing her staff a chance to take a break as well. Everyone except for Gabriela were planning some sort of trip of their own to take advantage of the free time off. But since she was staying on the island, Gabriela had agreed to stay at Quincy's house until Harold, who was the last dog to be picked up, went home on Tuesday.

"We'll have the guest room ready for you. Missy's just packing up now."

"No worries. You're leaving pretty early in the morning, yeah?"

Quincy nodded. "I'll feed this guy when I wake up and leave him in the house. So he'll just be here hanging out whenever you come by."

"Sure." Gabriela met Quincy's gaze. "Any idea where you're going yet?"

Quincy squinted. "Apparently there will be hiking. That's all I know so far."

The most conspiratorial grin spread across Gabriela's lips. "Oh, interesting."

"Wait a minute. Do you know?"

Gabriela squatted down and turned her attention to Harold. "Come here, boy."

"You do. You do know."

The smirk Gabriela flashed at Harold revealed the truth. And Quincy couldn't help but smile in response to this knowledge. Missy was making friends on the island. First Landry and now Gabriella. Quincy was glad. She wanted Missy to be happy and comfortable here.

Quincy said goodbye to Gabriela and Harold and took off down the trail toward town, still trying to outrun the desire flaming inside her. What would she do when she was trapped on a honeymoon with Missy 24/7?

****

Letting Missy choose their honeymoon location had been a momentary whim. But Quincy hadn't missed how important controlling her own fate was to Missy. So, Quincy had suggested Missy be in charge of the honeymoon. At the time, it had been easy to offer the simple gesture. But it had been killing her ever since.

Quincy was used to controlling everything: the show, her life, the details of how the dogs were cared for. She was the master of her daily routine. But now she was in Venezuela, following an itinerary set for her by a wife she barely knew. It took some getting used to. And if she was honest with herself, about five seconds after Missy had taken her offer and run with it, Quincy had been convinced that she would hate every moment of the honeymoon.

But she was very wrong.

When they took the flight to Caracas, Quincy still wasn't sure where the ultimate destination was. There were still so many possible destinations. She'd already been to a few places in South America. But Missy didn't know that. Would she disappoint her bride by not being thrilled to be back in Aruba, Bogota, or Panama City? Not that they weren't great places, but they weren't new. She could certainly be happy about the destination, but she wouldn't be able to fake unfamiliarity if that is what Missy was going for.

When they arrived at the final airport gate, and Missy revealed they were headed to Canaima National Park, Quincy was floored. It was perfect. Beyond perfect. She might have even chosen the destination herself had she bothered to give it any thought.

The remote park was filled with gorgeous landscapes, kayaking, hiking, and waterfalls, including the tallest waterfall in the world, Angel Falls, towering over 3,200 feet above the forest floor. It was the ultimate honeymoon destination for someone like her.

The travel to the lodge in Canaima had been stunning. The little plane puttered over thick jungle while Missy—her spiral locks in a riot around her shoulders—pressed her face to the window. Quincy alternated between looking at the scenery and appreciating the view of Missy caught up in excitement.

The lodge itself was rustic and quaint, but had everything they needed to be comfortable. It was a modern oasis in the jungle. Their single bungalow featured a king bed, a pull-out couch in a large living room, and a patio that opened up to a view of the Guianan Highlands dripping in green.

The cushy chaise Quincy now lounged in allowed a view of a tepui, its sheer rock face tainted in the red-orange glow of sunset. The sound of birds and monkeys calling out in the distance flowed over her like a wild symphony. She might have dozed off right there if something cold and wet hadn't touched the back of her hand.

Quincy jerked her head up to stare at Missy, who stood smiling, a tall margarita glass coated with condensation held out toward her. "Were you falling asleep?"

Quincy took the glass and shook her head, partly to clear the fog. "Not really."

Missy chuckled, the sound sweet and melodic. "I go and get drinks, and before I get back you're already asleep."

"It was a long day."

Missy pressed her lips together. "Well, if our two flights were long, you better rest up because we're going all the way to the falls, baby."

Quincy pointedly ignored the sensation that ran through her when Missy called her "baby" and took a drink of her margarita. It was smooth and tangy, with just a hint of sweet, the perfect match for her mood. "Angel Falls? We're going to Angel Falls?"

"Yes, of course. You didn't think we'd come all this way and not go?"

The playfulness in Missy's tone was completely new, and Quincy unexpectedly loved it. "It takes a couple days to get there, I hear."

"Yes. First, we'll spend a couple days at the resort. I have some hikes planned locally. Then we'll go on the trip to Angel Falls. After that trip, we'll come back here for the remainder of the honeymoon. The hotel will even keep the bungalow for us while we're gone."

Quincy leaned back in the chaise. She wouldn't mind a new bungalow, maybe one with two beds, but the rest of it sounded very good to her. She took another long sip of her drink.

"So, did I do good?" Missy asked.

Quincy could have heaped on well-deserved praise. Instead, she flashed a mischievous smirk and matched

Missy's playfulness. "It's a little too early to tell."

"Yeah, well. You look pretty happy."

"Maybe happy and tired look the same on me."

"You're not that tired."

"You forget, I'm old. Us old people don't travel as well as you young whipper snappers."

Missy scoffed.

"So what made you pick this place for the trip?"

Missy sat up in her lounger and swung her feet around so she was facing Quincy. She held her margarita glass cradled in her hands and gazed out at the lush forest. "I love national parks. My family has a cabin near Yosemite. They were always pretty casual about it. If left to their own devices, they would have gone maybe once a year. But I loved it there and would beg to go as often as possible when I was a kid. I took my first steps under Yosemite Falls, climbed El Capitan for the first time when I was fourteen, and basically grew up there. We also did a bit of traveling around the country and abroad, and I would always make sure a national park was on the itinerary. So when you told me to plan the honeymoon, I immediately started looking for national parks. It's just my go to, you know?"

Missy took a sip of her drink, then shifted her focus from the view to Quincy. "And I asked around to find out if you'd been to Canaima. Everyone seemed to think you hadn't. In fact, Jason said that you and he once had a conversation about how seeing Angel Falls was on both your bucket lists. So, I figured this would be a place we would both really enjoy. You like to trail run, I like to hike, and we both like cool drinks in a warm tropical environment; it seemed perfect."

"You really did your homework." Quincy tried desperately not to show how impressed she was with

Missy's gesture. It wasn't just that it was resourceful. It was thoughtful.

Missy shrugged and returned her gaze to the tepui. "I wanted it to be a good vacation. Uncle Jack says it's been a while since you've taken time off."

"He's not lying. I fully admit to being a workaholic. I built my business, and I want it to succeed. That means investing myself fully. And now with the show, I can't afford to let one slip for the other, so I have to work twice as hard. But I'm not abysmal at work-life balance. I always take the time to eat right and get my runs in." When she'd made that argument to Jack, he'd laughed at her and told her that was "bodily needs" balance, not "life" balance.

"My dad was that way before I was born. He was always home for dinner, even if he headed right back to work afterward. That time with my mom and brother was sacred. But other than dinner, they would do things all the time without him. Vacations, trips to see family. He was never there for any of that."

"What changed when you were born? He liked having a girl?"

"Sure. That's what he would say." A bright smile lit up Missy's face. "But it was more than that. My mom was older and had a few health problems. She wasn't planning to have any more kids. She thought they were all done. I was a bit of an oopsie. She had a hard pregnancy and an even harder delivery. We both almost died. My dad wasn't there for most of it. He arrived at the hospital just after my mom's heart had stopped. He was standing there in what he describes as the most petrifying state of shock when they got it started again."

Missy shrugged and pinned her gaze to Quincy. "I guess that changed everything. After that, he was with us all the time. Hired a couple people to do his job at the company and went part-time. He was there for every one of my childhood vacations. Never missed anything. I was lucky."

At that exact moment, Quincy's phone rang. She still wasn't certain why she'd assigned the high-pitched ringtone to Gina. And even though she hadn't heard it in over a year, she knew instantly who was calling. She hit the reject button and turned back to Missy. "Sorry. Your childhood sounds lovely." A familiar pain struck Quincy. But it was an old friend now, and she could feel it without it breaking her. Maybe she'd tell Missy about her parents one day.

"Like I said, I was lucky."

"And the being queer thing?"

"Not as easy. But I had Uncle Jack. And it's all water under the bridge now."

Quincy cleared her throat. "Well, I'm glad your childhood led to this great honeymoon." She held up her glass until Missy clinked it with her own.

"What about your family?" Missy asked. "Did you hike and run and camp with them? Are they where your love for nature comes from."

"We did some of that. I grew up in L.A., and we stayed in the city most of the time. But we would go out to the property on St. Croix at least once a year."

"Right. I remember that you said the property belonged to your family.

"Yes. I inherited it from my mother."

The way Missy's mouth turned down told Quincy she'd said too much. She didn't want to get into her parents' death and the hole it had left in her life. And she didn't need her fake bride to express sympathy over something that was an old wound anyway.

"But we don't need to talk about St. Croix right now. We're here." Quincy gestured around her. "I want to know about the hike you have planned for tomorrow. Get the map and show me."

When Missy got up and ducked into the room to retrieve the map, Quincy let out her breath. To get through these next two weeks, she'd have to avoid lingering on personal questions and the wonderfully soft angles of Missy's body. A feat that seemed more strenuous than any of the planned hikes.

Chapter 7

Stay Away from Romantic Settings

Missy had been nervous around boats since she fell off Uncle Jack's sailboat into the San Francisco Bay at eight years old. She largely avoided them since, especially the small, tippy ones. But if she wanted to get to Angel Falls, she'd have to spend hours on a boat, it was the only way to reach them.

This was part of the new adventure she was on, right? Try new things: move to an island, marry a famous dog trainer, visit the tallest waterfall in the world. Now was the time to embrace her bravery.

If only the boat wasn't quite so wobbly. She stared at the bobbing hull so long that she didn't even realize she and Quincy were the only tour guests not yet on the boat. All eyes were pinned to her. Their guide was holding out his hand and saying encouraging words that weren't really registering.

Quincy's hand landed on her back. She turned to see eyes crinkled at the corners, lips turned down. "Missy?"

She knew Quincy was about to tell her she didn't have to do this. That was the last thing she wanted to hear. She didn't want to be coddled. She didn't want her fear enabled. She was going to do this.

Before she could say something to head off Quincy's statement, Quincy pulled her one step away from the boat and held her finger out to the tour guide in a "give us a minute" gesture.

"Quincy, don't—"

"Missy, hear me out. I know you have a traumatic childhood incident that shaped your fear of boats. And I'm not telling you that it isn't important or significant." She turned Missy so they were face to face. "But you are not that little girl in the cold water anymore. You are a woman that goes after what she wants despite the barriers in her way. And you can and will get on that boat. And I'm going to be sitting right there next to you as you conquer this thing."

Never in her life had anyone said anything so perfect, so absolutely right that her knees nearly gave out, almost plummeting her to the ground. She locked them, tipped her chin, and stared her wife in the eyes. "Let's do this."

****

Water poured over Missy's skin with the perfect amount of pressure. It didn't sting, nor was it a gentle trickle. It hit her neck and shoulders with a massaging force that made her groan.

This small waterfall at the edge of the lagoon was a miniscule version of the majestic Angel Falls they'd seen three days ago. Now that they were back at the resort, they were undertaking tamer adventures, and this spot was perfect.

Because her head was thrown back, the waterproof camera pointed toward her wasn't in her line of sight. But she knew it was there, capturing her ecstasy as the water flowed over her. If the lens was catching her torso, the waterline hitting her just below her belly button would at least prevent it from seeing her flower-print bikini bottoms, but it would still provide an ample view of her stomach stretching up to the skimpy matching top.

She kept her eyes closed and tried not to think too hard about that. It was easier to pretend her body, her expressions, and the emotions she couldn't keep contained, weren't being recorded to eventually be broadcast to anyone who might care to see what the famous dog trainer and her new wife were up to.

Missy tilted her head back down; her hair heavy with water. Stepping away from the waterfall, she opened her eyes. Swiping at her face quickly with her hands, she focused her gaze on Quincy.

Camera held up, smile beaming, mist from the waterfall clinging to the smooth skin on her face, Quincy was an incredible sight. She glanced up from the camera's view finder. Her smile changed a little, wobbling, then shifting into something less genuine.

Missy stepped forward, gliding through the water. Her bare feet squished in the sand, moving uphill as she left the ditch carved by the falls. By the time she reached her wife, her bikini bottoms were fully exposed to the air, but it was warm and humid enough that it didn't cause her to shiver.

She reached out toward the camera. "Your turn."

Quincy handed over the equipment even as she shook her head and laughed. "Oh no. You're not filming me under a waterfall."

Missy clicked the record button and pointed the lens at Quincy. "Who said anything about the falls? I'm just taking video of my sexy wife in the water."

Missy's words were nothing but the truth. Quincy wore a tankini with boy shorts. Technically, far more of her skin was covered than Missy's—but the sleek lines of muscle, the curvy shape of her torso, the absolutely perfect ass—it was all there for Missy to appreciate.

The sensation of attraction had been growing inside her for weeks now. And with Quincy just inches away wearing a wet, navy and white striped bathing suit that clung to every part of her body, Missy's nerves were on fire.

Concentrating on producing footage for Myra was the only way to control her libido. She had to plan, script, and act out the perfect 'happy couple' video, which would hopefully keep her from throwing herself at her new wife in the middle of a waterfall pool in a national park.

The audience helped, too. Missy swiveled the camera to reveal the scene, three couples at various locations around the pool. Two were under the waterfall. One was young. A beautiful woman with an impossibly handsome man holding her waist as she laughed. The other couple was an adorable husband and wife in their retirement years, holding hands as they waded toward the falling water. On the shore, relaxing on the sand, were two women, a smaller one enveloped in the other's arms in the exact way Missy wanted to be cuddled into Quincy.

After the three-sixty swing of the camera, Missy focused back on the stunning woman in front of her. "How's the honeymoon so far, Quincy?"

When they were filming the show back on St. Croix, something always came over Quincy when the cameras rolled, a change in her expression. Uncle Jack called it her acting face. The transition was clear to everyone on set. Missy fully expected Quincy to turn that on now.

But she didn't. There was no sign of Quincy-in-performance-mode. Instead, she wore the same expression she'd held while watching Missy bathe in the waterfall. Her lips turned up at the corners just a tiny bit. Her eyes sparkled. Her features were soft; her shoulders relaxed. She was not wearing her acting face. Not at all.

"Well, Missy, since you asked. I'm having a great honeymoon. And it's especially fun because everything we've been doing is a complete surprise."

"You didn't know a thing about it, did you?"

"No. I didn't. I let my new wife plan the whole thing."

Missy's stomach flipped when Quincy said that word "wife."

"And how did I do?"

Quincy swiveled her head to glance around at the waterfall, the crystal blue pool, and the impossibly green jungle in the background, then turned back to Missy. "Not bad. Not bad at all."

Missy took a step forward. Ripples of water she created in her wake traveled to Quincy, hitting her thighs and spreading out to dissipate in the far reaches of the pool. "Not bad? Is that really what you think? We've seen the tallest waterfall in the world. Taken some of the most beautiful hikes imaginable, and stayed in an amazing jungle bungalow for a week, and it's 'not bad'? Really?"

Quincy laughed, throwing her head back. Her short locks flew in the misty air. When she met Missy's gaze again, her eyes shone with a new brightness, one Missy had only seen a few times, all of them on this trip. That look showed up at the base of Angel Falls, at the top of a tepui they'd climbed, and right now, gazing at Missy in this little pool.

"You did good, Missy. Real good."

Missy took another step forward, bringing her too close to Quincy to be able to properly film. She hit the stop button and dropped the camera so it hung around her neck. Her newly freed hands floated at the top of the pristine water, itching to reach out and touch Quincy.

"I'm glad you like it." Missy's words were so soft she wasn't entirely certain Quincy could hear her over the roar of the waterfall.

Quincy tilted her head, making Missy think she hadn't heard. But then she lifted one hand and placed it gently on Missy's cheek. It was the first time Quincy had ever touched her face. Missy leaned into the touch, desperate for more, but afraid to ask.

Then, as if a bubble had been burst by a sharp pin, Quincy pulled her hand away from Missy and took a step back. Her eyes shifted, and her lips turned down.

"I'm getting cold." Quincy moved quickly, passing Missy to head toward the shore.

The temperature of the water almost matched the air, and being cold seemed unlikely. But Missy didn't take the time to really absorb Quincy's words. Instead, she moved to keep up as Quincy made her way to the river's edge. She managed to hit the beach just a few inches behind Quincy, following her to the spot where they'd left their big beach bag stuffed with towels, water bottles, and sunscreen.

Quincy pulled out a towel and wrapped herself tightly in it before dropping onto the ground. Missy took longer to dry her body, then wrap her hair. Then she plopped down beside Quincy.

"Are you warmer?" Missy asked.

"Yeah. For sure." Quincy didn't look at her. Instead, she kept her gaze trained on the waterfall.

Missy felt a chill now herself, the same one that descended upon them every night before bed, when Missy found herself alone in the big king with Quincy huddled up on the pull-out couch. It was a little early in the day for this routine, but Missy sighed and accepted it for what it was.

"Hi there!"

It took Missy a moment to locate the person who

belonged to the voice calling out to them. But her gaze finally found an adorable redhead, tiny and cute, nestled in the arms of a tall beauty with long, flowing dreads. It was the couple she'd seen sitting on shore when she'd scanned the area from the water, but she hadn't realized how close they'd landed to them on the beach.

"Hey," Missy said, her voice easily traversing the twenty or thirty feet between where they were seated.

"On your honeymoon?" the redhead asked.

"Yeah, you?"

"No. Five year anniversary. But we could tell you were newlyweds."

Given that Missy felt more like the awkward kid from high school unwillingly shoved into the friend corner, she couldn't help but feed her curiosity. What did this stranger see? "How's that?"

It was the dark-haired woman who answered this time. "You look like you'll die if you don't get back to the hotel soon."

The redhead giggled.

Missy beamed. She wasn't the only one who'd seen something on Quincy's face in the water, something that meant she wasn't completely alone in her feelings. Two strangers had glimpsed it too.

She turned to see what she could find now on Quincy's face. What would this observation force her to confront?

Quincy's pinched lips and squinted eyes moved quickly, darting around as she shot to her feet. "We should actually get back." She waved at the couple, a fake smile plastered on her face. "I'm going to head to the bungalow." And before Missy could even stand up, Quincy was marching away from her.

****

Missy opened the door to the bungalow to find Quincy barreling toward her with an armload of clothing. Quincy stopped before they had a head-on collision. A pair of women's boxers escaped the tangle of fabrics and floated down to land on her sandaled foot. Quincy shifted her gaze to stare at it like it had offended her.

"What are you doing?"

"Laundry. I'm fresh out."

Missy picked up Quincy's underwear and tucked it into the pile in her arms. She couldn't possibly be out of clothes. Missy had just used the hotel's laundry service two days ago, and half the clothes in Quincy's arms she was sure hadn't been worn. "Do you have to do it now?"

"It's the best time, get it in before dinner."

"We're still going to the resort restaurant, right? I made reservations."

"Yeah. Of course." Quincy squeezed around Missy in the entryway and put her hand on the doorknob. "I'll be back in a couple hours."

Before Missy could argue, Quincy was gone. Missy dropped the beach bag on the dresser and sat on the edge of the bed. Something was going on with Quincy. Not only was she doing laundry that didn't need to be done, but she was also planning to stay away from the room and hang out in the small laundry room no more than a few hundred yards from the bungalow rather than coming back in between. Which begged the question, why was she avoiding Missy?

She glanced over at the couch that pulled out into a spare bed. They'd stopped folding it back up before housekeeping came by. Why bother hiding that you aren't sharing a bed to strangers who probably didn't care anyway? So there it sat, all day long, made up as a bed, a stark reminder that they were definitely, absolutely not having sex. Missy turned away from the offending furniture and headed out onto the patio.

She got through several chapters of a new book before Quincy reappeared, a stack of neatly folded clothes in her arms. They had to move quickly if they were to make their reservations, but she sat still in her location on the patio. She wanted to make Quincy come to her. But her ploy didn't work, and Quincy ended up calling out to her that they had to leave instead. Missy sighed and followed her bride out of the bungalow.

As they got situated at their table, Missy reflected that no couple could ask for a more romantic setting. It was probably why Missy and Quincy had avoided this restaurant so far. Moonlight illuminated the colorful waters of Canaima Lagoon. Their seat on the restaurant porch sat above a leveled area on the beach that some guests were using as a dance floor. The band was located in the perfect spot for moving to the beat, but far enough away that diners could still hold a conversation.

Which would have been great if they were capable of conversation. But at the moment, this married couple was not doing a good job of looking the part. Missy sipped at her wine, glancing at Quincy over the rim of the glass. As soon as Missy's gaze hit her, Quincy turned away, giving Missy a view of her cheek as she examined the dance floor.

After their server took their food order and left them, the awkward silence continued until Missy couldn't take it any longer. She reached across the table and touched Quincy's arm. Quincy jumped but then tried to cover with a smile.

"I think that's the couple we saw at the river today." She pointed to the two unmistakable figures whose words had sent Quincy running for an excuse to not interact with her wife.

"Yeah. I guess so."

Until today, their trip had been relatively free of awkward moments. Missy and Quincy had been co-workers on a great adventure, so consumed with activity they barely had time to talk, let alone confront attractions, emotions, or anything complicated like that. But under that waterfall the earth had tilted. The air between them became thick with desire. And when that couple on the beach voiced the palpable tension—so obvious it could be seen by strangers across the distance—Quincy had changed instantly.

Now here they were, blanketed in silence, watching a real happy couple tangle their limbs together in the most romantic setting Missy had ever seen. She racked her brain for something to say that would cut through the tension. But before she could, the server returned with a plate of appetizers. Since shoving food in her mouth seemed a good way to deal with the moment, she reached out to take one. But Quincy did the same thing at the same moment, and their hands met.

Missy retreated just as quickly as Quincy did, both acting as if they'd been burned. But then Quincy smiled and let out a soft chuckle. "It looks good, doesn't it?"

"Oh, for sure."

Quincy gestured for Missy to go first. She grabbed one of the pastelitos and took a bite. As soon as the savory, cheesy, fried pastry hit her tongue she let out a long, low moan. She peered over at Quincy, expecting to see her grabbing a bite of her own. Instead, she met wide eyes. Quincy's tongue peeked out and licked her bottom lip as she watched Missy.

Something bloomed in Missy's chest as she held

Quincy's gaze. Until finally, Quincy broke the connection, focusing her attention back on the plate of food. "Good, huh?"

Missy wasn't entirely sure what the subject of that question was. But no matter what, she had the same answer. "Yes."

They ate in silence, gazes clashing over and over again until every crumb was gone. Quincy leaned back in her chair. "We haven't even had the main course yet, and I'm already feeling like I'm going to have to go for a long run tomorrow."

"It's your vacation. You don't have to pay for your sins." As soon as the words left her mouth, Missy realized how spicy they sounded. And she didn't care. She'd take those words to heart. It was her honeymoon, and she was tired of walking on eggshells. "But I do have an idea that will burn some calories."

"Oh yeah, what's that?"

Missy held Quincy's gaze, unflinching. "Let's dance. I'm sure there is time for one song before dinner comes."

She expected an argument. But Quincy quickly agreed. She stood and headed for the dance floor. Shocked by the response, it took Missy a moment to move, and she had to jog to catch up with Quincy as her longer legs marched down the steps of the deck to the beach.

Quincy dumped her sandals near a pile of the other dancers' discarded footwear, picked a relatively empty spot amongst them, and turned to wait for Missy. Missy's sandals had straps and it took a moment longer to wrestle her way out of them. Once she did, she practically ran across the sand to Quincy, an unrelenting grin pasted on her face. This was really happening!

Quincy accepted Missy into her arms, resting her hands on Missy's waist while Missy looped her arms over

Quincy's shoulders. They came together naturally, just as they had when they'd share that kiss on her uncles' deck weeks ago.

Missy's legs were bare beneath her short dress and slid against Quincy's, whose own shorts allowed the skin of their thighs to meet, creating sparks between them. Their hips pressed together, and their bodies swayed in a way that ignited sensations deep inside Missy's most intimate places.

Missy reveled in the movement, completely losing herself. Like a being made only of her senses, she swam in the warmth of touch, the oatmeal and orchid scent of Quincy, the sound of Quincy's breathing in her ear, the taste of the pastelitos they'd shared lingering in her mouth.

And then it all stopped. Like a car coming screeching to a halt, everything ended in a terrible crash as Quincy moved away. Her absence sent a chill through Missy. Her eyes flew open just in time to see Quincy's back as she walked away toward the water of Canaima Lagoon.

Missy's shoulders dropped as if her wrists were tied to cement blocks. The beautiful intimate moment collapsed, leaving her cold and alone on the beach. She turned her gaze away from Quincy's retreating figure, and it snagged onto the bright green eyes of the redheaded woman. Like a specter of pain, this woman and her partner just kept popping up when Missy was in the midst of Quincy's rejection.

There was no doubt pity behind those eyes, and if she looked around, she'd see it elsewhere, too. The dance floor was practically still. People watched her, the woman alone, her wife having fled as if she were a terrible pariah.

The embarrassment was nearly as bad as the rejection. But out of the two, it was the easier one to focus on in the moment. Welcome almost. So Missy walked slowly, rather than running, weaving her way through the couples toward the stairs leading to the restaurant.

An older woman smiled sweetly as she passed. The man dancing with her winked in that cute grandpa way. Another couple turned their stares away, focusing intently on one another as she moved by them. But when she reached the redhead, she felt an arm touch her shoulder.

She stopped beside the couple, who were no longer moving at all, but instead both turned toward her. "Are you all right?" The redhead asked.

Missy tipped her head in an attempt stave off the tears that threatened to fall. "Yeah. Just a little lover's spat. You know how it goes on a honeymoon."

"We do," the redhead's partner said.

"Can we help?"

"No. Thank you, though. Just enjoy yourselves. We'll be all right."

Missy continued her trek. She made it up onto the restaurant platform, paid the bill for their meal and asked for the food to be delivered in to-go containers to their room. Then she took the short walk back to the bungalow without spilling a single tear.

By the time she was alone in their room, exhaustion and loneliness tied for first place in the race of unhappiness in her mind. Which meant there was only one thing to do.

Chapter 8

Avoid Seeing Your Fake Spouse Naked

Quincy had long ago come to terms with the fact that she was a runner. It was undeniable. It's why she was living on an island nearly three thousand miles from home. It's why she'd gotten into a fake marriage with her assistant rather than confront her ex. And it was definitely why she ran from the dance floor where she'd been intimately intertwined with said wife.

Sand squished through her toes as she walked along the edge of the lagoon where water met land. The muted light from the restaurant barely touched her here. She moved slowly down the beach, trying to keep from plowing into some unseen object. The sound of the band had faded, and her only company was the sloshing water lapping lazily against the shore.

Her life had been full, and she'd had her share of intimate moments with beautiful women. But none of it held a candle to that one short dance with Missy. No gratuitous sex could conjure up the flame of desire those innocent touches had ignited.

Quincy shook her head and pulled her phone from her pocket. Grateful she had reception, she dialed Olivia's number.

"Hey newlywed!" Her best friend's voice was cheerful.

"Hey."

"What's wrong? I can hear the sad-ass tone of your

voice. Is it because the gig is up?"

"Gig? What gig?"

"Your family totally knows about the wedding. I got a call from, like, all of them."

This threw Quincy out of her original melancholy and into this new problem. "Really? Why the hell haven't they said anything to me?"

"They're waiting for you to tell them yourself."

This was a problem she didn't have the head space for. "I can't with them right now. I literally just ran away from my bride."

Olivia chuckled. "Ran away how? I mean are we talking about in the middle of…ya know?"

"No! We were just dancing. I told you it's a fake marriage."

"Hey, don't forget that I watch your show. Your new wife was on the episode that just dropped, and she is smoking hot. I mean super-duper hot. And straight-up your type. So don't pretend with me."

Quincy let out a breath. This is why people had best friends. "That's the problem. I'm attracted to her."

"I cannot for the life of me figure out why being attracted to your new wife is a problem. Girl, enjoy that honeymoon!"

"No. Olivia. Stop. You know I can't do that. This is fake marriage. She's helping me out. I'm not going to take advantage of that."

"Okay. Wait. What do you mean 'take advantage of'?"

"I mean what I mean."

"The person I saw on your show was a grown-ass woman that is perfectly capable of entering into a consensual sexual relationship and making up her own damn mind about whether or not she wants to get down and dirty with her wife."

Quincy stopped her forward motion on the beach. She couldn't deny any of that. Because it wasn't really the point anyway. She'd been lying to herself.

"You know I'm right," Olivia continued. "You're making the decision for her. But that's bullshit. She can make up her own mind."

Of course that was true. In fact, the way Missy asserted her agency was one of the things Quincy found so attractive about her. No, this was about her fear. Fear she'd get attached. She did not want a real relationship. She did not want feelings.

She spun around and faced the restaurant. It was too far in the distance now to see more than the faint glow from the lights. But Missy was there somewhere, rejected and alone. Quincy's abject fear and failure to recognize it for what it was had done that. What an asshole.

"If you want her, why don't you tell her that and let her decide if it's appropriate or not to get her sexy on with you?"

Because Quincy was pretty sure Missy would agree. Then she'd have to worry about if a sexual relationship would lead to more. But the realization was too new. She couldn't say any of that, not even to Olivia. "I don't know."

"You don't know?"

"No." Quincy started heading back toward the resort without any purposeful thought about it.

"Quincy, my dear. You better figure it out. Because you have a week to go, sweetie. And if it was me, I'd have been trying to convince that beauty to consummate the marriage from the first night."

"I think I need to figure my shit out."

"Yes, honey. You do."

Quincy said a quick goodbye to Olivia, tucked her

phone into her pocket, and ran back toward the resort. As the restaurant started to come back into view, she could make out figures on the dance floor and spotted the couple from the waterfall. Aside from them, all the rest were male/female pairings. The stunning training assistant she'd married a month ago was not among them.

Why had she thought Missy would still be standing there waiting for her? Of course she wasn't. She had surely left. But the question was, where had she gone? To their room? To the bar to get comfort from a sexy stranger? And why was she being so obnoxious about this? Like some jealous wife.

She mentally cataloged another new realization; she wanted Missy all to herself.

****

The bungalow was eerily quiet. Missy must not be here. Next stop was the resort bar. It seemed like a logical place for Missy to go when her wife was being an unreasonable twat.

Quincy was pivoting on her feet to head out when she heard splashing water coming from behind the bathroom door. "Missy?"

"Yeah? I'm here."

Quincy moved quickly to the bathroom door and pressed her forehead against the cream-colored wood. "Hey, um. Can we talk?"

A long pause greeted her question; her heart caught in her throat as she waited. Then she heard Missy's quiet reply. "Sure. Come in."

Quincy took two deep breaths before opening the door. The warmth of the room hit her at the same moment her body lit on fire from the sight of Missy laid out in the tub.

It wasn't like on television. No strategically placed bubbles shielded Missy's body from view.

No, Quincy had a good view of it all.

She forced her eyes to stay focused on Missy's face. Damp hair clung to wet cheeks. Deep brown eyes peered back at Quincy. God she was beautiful.

"Hi."

"Hi." Missy's smile was soft and sweet. Way better than Quincy deserved.

"I fucked up."

Missy laughed, and Quincy's shoulders dropped. "Yeah. You did. You ran off without saying a word. What, exactly, did I do wrong?"

Quincy took a step closer. "Nothing. You didn't do anything wrong."

Missy stared up at her, waiting for an explanation. But Quincy had no idea what to say. "I was just having a moment."

Missy tipped her head. "About what?"

Quincy ran a hand through her hair. She was suddenly sweating. "The thing is, when we entered into this deal, we didn't talk about intimacy."

"What about intimacy?"

"Whether we should have it or not."

"I see. We should talk about that."

Quincy crouched down beside the tub and sat on the bathmat facing Missy. The lip of porcelain created a welcome separation that kept her from seeing Missy's body under the water.

"So, let's talk about it." Missy laid her arm on the edge of the bathtub, her hand held out toward Quincy.

Quincy took the offering, matching the posture with her own arm on the tub in the opposite direction. Her palm met Missy's, and their fingers intertwined. "I suppose we should have had this conversation before we got married."

"Not sure it would have made sense then."

So, Missy felt it too. She must have. The building attraction between them, like magnets growing stronger with time. "I suppose not. But here we are now."

Missy squeezed Quincy's hand. "Yes. Here we are."

Quincy stared into those brown eyes and the truth poured out of her. "I talked to Olivia about all of this."

"Your friend from back home?"

"Yeah. We've been friends since middle school. We both came out to our parents at the same time during a neighborhood barbeque."

Missy smiled. "You told me that story last week on one of our hikes."

"She's pretty different from me in a lot of ways."

"It kind of sounded that way from your stories."

"She's very straightforward about things. I tend to beat around the bush."

Amusement danced in Missy's eyes as she watched Quincy doing exactly that at this very moment. "Um, hm."

"The thing is, I initially wanted to keep our relationship completely professional. It's just simpler that way."

"It is simpler. And to be honest, I thought we could do that too."

"But not anymore?"

"Definitely not anymore."

That little statement snapped the strings tying Quincy in knots. She leaned forward, brought her free hand up, and slid it behind Missy's head, cupping her drenched curls. She closed the space between their mouths, sealing them together in one swift motion. Missy reacted by parting her lips and darting out her tongue. Quincy accepted the invitation, groaning into the kiss.

Wrestling with the desire to throw herself into the tub, Quincy pulled back but kept her forehead pressed against Missy's. If she wasn't careful, she'd let her overwhelming want trample all common sense. She couldn't afford a morning after filled with regret. They were married and stuck together in the middle of the jungle for another six days. They didn't need more awkwardness right now.

"Are you absolutely sure?"

"Yes. But, I'm also nervous."

Quincy's head shot back. She stared at Missy, examining her face. Her lip was trapped between her teeth, her cheeks pink.

Quincy might have hang-ups. But one thing she didn't have was nerves, not when it came to sex. She needed to understand. "Why? Why would you be nervous?"

Missy shrugged. "I mean, it's normal right?"

Quincy stood suddenly, breaking all connections between them. Missy stood just as quickly, water spraying out as she displaced it. Wet and naked in front of her, Missy's expression shifted. "I think it's okay to be nervous."

Completely unable to think rationally with Missy's naked body like an elephant in a broom closet taking up every available thought in her brain, Quincy fumbled her hands over the shelf to her right, grabbed a towel, and shoved it at Missy. Then she took a step back, placing herself in the doorway of the small room.

Missy wrapped the towel around her torso and stepped out of the tub. Water sluiced off her and onto the mat Quincy had just been sitting on, soaking it the same way this conversation had dampened the mood between them.

But Quincy still had to know. "Why? Why do I make

you nervous?"

"I didn't say that it was you making me nervous." Missy straightened her spine, holding Quincy's gaze. "It's a long story, and I'm not really inclined to tell it when I'm standing here in a towel. But my sexual experience is limited. I'm…"

"You're what?"

Missy took in a deep breath, her shoulders rising and falling. Whatever she was about to say was going to be a lot. Quincy could feel it.

"I'm demisexual."

At first Quincy was distracted trying to remember the exact nuances of demisexuality. When she pulled up that file in her brain, she took another step backward. "So, you only feel sexual attraction once you've already developed feelings for someone."

"Basically, yeah."

Missy had made it clear she was attracted to Quincy, and their conversation had Quincy thinking they could have a casual sexual fling. It would be nothing more than a perk of their fake marriage. But this changed everything.

Missy took a step toward her, and Quincy held up her hands. "Maybe we should put the brakes on."

"Because of how I identify?" Missy furrowed her brow. "Pardon me, but that's bullshit."

"I just think this dynamic complicates things, and we should take a step back and think it through first." That was logical, right? No one wanted to make a mistake in this situation.

"My identity is a complication." Missy held the towel to her chest with one hand as she leaned toward Quincy, her face turning redder by the second, her eyes lit with fire.

"You're mad."

"You're brilliant."

Quincy kept moving back until she was fully out of the bathroom. "Maybe I should leave. Just for a little bit until we've both had time to cool down."

"Fine, Quincy. Sounds good. Run away again." Missy waved her hand toward the door.

Quincy searched for something else to say that could diffuse the argument. But she came up with nothing. The expression on Missy's face told her that she was out of options. Leaving would make tomorrow awkward again, but it was better than what was happening now. "Okay. I'll leave for tonight. But I'll be back in the morning. Okay?"

Missy turned back toward the bathroom. "Fine. Works for me." She shut the bathroom door behind her, effectively shutting Quincy out.

Quincy grabbed a bag that was still half-packed and scrambled for the door. Keeping her focus on her breathing, she stepped carefully along the stone path from the bungalow to the main building.

The front desk only had one occupant at this time of night, a sweet-faced young woman with long, brown hair and bright pink lipstick. Quincy approached her and improvised a story on the spot. "My wife thinks she's coming down with a cold, and she's worried about giving it to me. So I wanted to see if you have an extra room."

The woman's face immediately flooded with concern. "Oh, no. Should I send some tea to her room?"

"No, thank you. She doesn't want to expose anyone. I already made sure she has everything she needs. But she really doesn't want me sleeping there tonight. Do you have something else?"

"Yes. We always keep a spare room for emergencies."

She clicked a few keys on her computer. "And it's available. Though," she looked up at Quincy and frowned, "I'm afraid it's not a bungalow. It's a small room here in the main building. Just a bed and a bathroom."

"That will be just fine."

The woman did a few more things on her computer and handed Quincy a key with a kind smile. "I hope your wife feels better soon."

"Me, too." Quincy's stomach sank as she turned away, the key to her room burning in her palm, exactly where just minutes ago, she'd held Missy's hand.

Following the placards hung on the wall, she moved through the cavernous tiled space until she located a narrow hallway. Beside the vending machines sat a lone door, its appearance battered and sad, not unlike her mood.

Using the key, Quincy unlocked the door and stepped inside. Pine-scented cleaner assaulted her nose. Along a windowless wall sat a small bed covered in a muted tan spread and piled with crisp, white pillows. She stared at it with trepidation, her back pressed against the door. This was worse than sleeping on the pull-out couch in their bungalow. At least in the shared space she could hear Missy's breathing from across the room, make out her silhouette in the dark, and know she was there.

Quincy had grown accustomed to living alone after she moved to the island, but had quickly gotten used to Missy's comforting company. This sad room plunged her into an unfamiliar loneliness. With a sigh, she heaved herself away from the door, marching toward her fate and the forsaken little bed.

Chapter 9

Beware of Jealousy

Missy squinted her eyes. Was this even real? The colors on the lagoon were stunning. Oranges and reds blended perfectly with blue, aqua, and green. She moved toward the group of a dozen people on the beach who had clearly just started gathering near a boat. Not far away, another set of tourists were exiting a different canoe that had just pulled up to the shore.

Missy patted herself on the back for not having booked the morning Lagoon tour. The bottle of wine she drank after Quincy left had rendered Missy pretty useless that morning. She'd still been a hot mess a few hours ago when that tour left.

Even now, after a light lunch, she wasn't sure she was up to an afternoon of tourist activities, especially one involving a boat. But she'd booked this ahead of time, and if nothing else, Missy had to show up so she could see if her wife did too.

Despite Quincy's promise to connect in the morning, she'd heard nothing from her. She suspected Quincy had gone trail running and lost track of time. But Missy refused to be the one to reach out first. Quincy said she'd come back. It was her responsibility.

Scanning the group as she approached, Missy did see a familiar face. It wasn't the high cheekbones, sharp chin, and complex, hazel eyes of her wife. It was the redhead they'd seen at the beach and again on the dance floor last night. But there was no sign of her partner anywhere.

The tour guide gave a small speech letting everyone know what to expect and how to be safe on their journey to see the falls at the edge of the lagoon. He explained that when they got to the other side of the lagoon, they would be leaving the boat and hiking to a waterfall. He emphasized the importance of having a hiking buddy for safety.

Missy suppressed an internal groan. Way to twist the knife, dude.

When he was done, the crowd began to load onto the large dugout canoe balanced on the sand. Its rear end bobbed in the lake waters, making Missy's stomach churn. This boat was even smaller than the one they'd taken to Angel Falls, and for that trip she'd had Quincy at her side, giving her calming reassurance.

Only Quincy wasn't here now.

Missy bobbed as one foot was raised above the other by the shifting surface below her. Somehow, in the middle of her brooding, she'd managed to step onboard the boat. She followed directions and found herself in the rear with the redhead sitting beside her.

"Hi!" the woman said.

Missy swallowed hard as the boat rocked. "Hi."

The woman stuck out her hand, pale and covered in delicate freckles. "I'm Penny. I think I saw you and your partner on the beach yesterday."

Missy appreciated that Penny didn't mention the far more humiliating encounter they had on the dance floor.

"My wife and I, yeah. You did. I'm Missy."

"It looks like you're alone today, too. And a fellow American! So, I hope you don't mind if I make you my hiking partner." Penny blinked, and her bright green eyes were so warm and welcoming, Missy instantly felt more comfortable.

"My wife wasn't feeling well." Missy would have kicked herself if she could. Why did she feel the need to explain? Especially when they both knew what happened last night. She could have just stayed quiet.

But the lie was out there now, and Penny clamped onto it. "Oh, no. That is such a bummer when you're on vacation. Your honeymoon, right?"

Yep. Shitty, shitty honeymoon. "Yeah. You?"

"Nah. We've been married for five years." It was the same thing they'd said by the waterfall. But Penny repeated it as if that brief exchange had never happened. And Missy was grateful. "We're not newlyweds anymore. Just on a trip. Linda had a work event in Caracas. So she added a few days on either side, and we made a vacation of it. She's at the thing in town now. And I'm just trying to stay busy until she gets back."

Missy smiled at her. She wished her own situation was as easy to explain. Maybe her pre-emptive lie had been a good move. How could she possibly explain the convoluted conversation she and Quincy had that started with them planning a night of sex and ended with Quincy staying in a separate room?

"Well, I'm happy to be your hiking partner." Missy flashed what she hoped was a comforting and friendly smile.

Penny grinned back, an adorable dimple lighting up her right cheek. "Thanks." She let out a sigh. "I almost didn't come. I hate being a stranger."

Missy chuckled. "I know what you mean. I just moved to St. Croix from San Francisco and feel like that every day."

"San Francisco? We live in San Diego!"

"That's great."

"And now you live in St. Croix?"

"Yeah. Have you ever been?"

The canoe ride passed with conversation like that. Where they were from. What they did. Penny was a nurse, and her wife, Linda, was some sort of civil consultant. How they liked Canaima. It was beautiful and adventurous. And on and on. It was easy small talk between a couple of strangers with a lot in common sitting on a boat in a lagoon in the opposite hemisphere from their home.

The constant chatting, and the effort it took to keep it up, helped Missy escape the whirling thoughts she'd been caught up in since last night as well as the fear that clung to her from the moment she stepped up to the swaying boat. The hike felt good, too. Walking along with Penny at the back of the pack, she engaged in easy conversation while soaking in the greens, blues, and reds, like paint splattered across an already stunning landscape.

The end of the trail featured a breathtaking view from behind the curtain of a waterfall. The rushing water, so loud it drowned out all other sounds, seemed to wash away Missy's anger and confusion from the night before, leaving only sadness and longing in its place. As much as she appreciated Penny's company, she would have loved to be standing here with Quincy right now.

The ride back was quieter. She had apparently not been the only one affected by the falls. Conversation on the boat overall was soft and sparse. In contrast to their ride out, Penny was quiet and introspective. It gave Missy room to reflect on her own changed mood.

When she landed back on shore, Missy checked her phone, but there was nothing from Quincy. No "sorry I bailed on our plans." No explanation about how she'd meant to come but lost track of the time. Nothing. Hope threatened to fade away like the thin stream of smoke rising from an extinguished flame.

"Hey, Missy."

Stopping in her tracks Missy spun around. She'd started walking back toward the lodge without any parting words to her hiking partner.

"Oh, sorry." Embarrassed by her rudeness, she took a step back toward Penny. "I was lost in thought." She smiled apologetically. "That trip was amazing. I probably need a nap now."

"Me, too." Penny ran a hand through her hair. "I just wondered if you would join me for dinner. Your wife, too, if she's feeling up to it. I'm just…" Penny shrugged.

Lonely. Missy got it. More than Penny would know. "Yes. Of course. I would love to."

"Great. Meet me at the hotel restaurant in say two hours?"

"Yeah. I'll be there."

Missy waved goodbye to her new friend. And for the first time since Quincy walked out the night before, she stepped a little lighter. If her wife was going to abandon her, she'd make the best of her vacation anyway.

****

Vacation didn't mean just one thing to Missy. It could be a sweaty hike in the jungle or a relaxing sun-soaked lounge on the beach. It could also mean putting on a cute dress, strappy sandals, and red lipstick and going out to a nice dinner.

She liked enjoying the moment, and that's what she intended to do now. Sluffing off the tangle of emotions she'd been steeped in for twenty-four hours, she took a last look at herself in the full-length mirror hanging on the bathroom door.

She looked good. And that was for her. It boosted her confidence and lifted her spirits. A genuine smile spread across her lips. She pulled open the bathroom door, ready to head to the restaurant to meet Penny. But she barely made it out when she stopped. Feet planted on the hardwood floor, she stared straight ahead at Quincy.

Quincy stood just inside the bungalow's front door, hands shoved into the pockets of her thin vest. Her eyes roamed Missy from the leather sandals and painted toenails to the flowery A-line dress, to her hair, blow dried and brushed out until it bounced along her shoulders.

"Going somewhere?"

How was that the first thing Quincy said to her? Not, *hey sorry I didn't come back like I promised.* Or *let's talk.* Or even, *you look amazing.* Missy pressed her lips together for a second before shrugging her shoulders. "I don't know. Maybe. Did you expect me to be still sitting in the tub waiting for you to return?"

Quincy's eyes widened. Missy stepped toward the bed and retrieved her purse, slinging it over her shoulder. Then she stared Quincy down. "I'm going to be late. And you're in my way."

Quincy ran her hand over her short hair. It feathered in the wake of her fingers. A few sparks of grey peeked out. Missy found those subtle hints at age sexy as hell, but she'd never tell Quincy that.

"I'm sorry about the way things went down last night."

"Went down. Way to own your mistakes." Every bit of confidence Missy had ever owned in her whole life was saved up inside her, waiting to spill out at this very moment. She needed it to, because she'd set Quincy up on a pedestal. And the only way they could be equals was for her to tear that pedestal down and force Quincy to see her eye-to-eye.

"You're right. I fucked up last night. I was being unreasonable. And I should have come back sooner today. I ended up on a long hike, thinking, you know?"

"Sure. That's what I did on the canoe ride, alone."

Quincy threw her head back. "Shit. I forgot about that. Did you do okay on the boat?"

"Too late to worry about that now, Quincy. Please step out of my way."

But Quincy still didn't move. Missy stomped toward her, hoping a game of chicken might work. But she flinched first, stopping just inches away. Quincy lifted a hand and placed it on her shoulder. Her voice was gentle, tender even. "Where are you going?"

"To dinner."

"Alone? I mean, you don't have to eat alone. I could go with you."

"No. Not alone. With a friend."

Quincy's face was as transparent as a freshly washed window. Her eyes were wide, nostrils flared, lips pressed tight. "A friend?"

"Yes, someone I met on the tour you bailed on this morning."

Quincy's shoulders fell, her facial features softened. Her hand moved from Missy's shoulder to her neck. "I'm sorry about that. I should have been there." She leaned forward and kissed Missy. Her lips were soft and sweet. Apology echoed through the tenderness in her mouth.

It almost worked. Missy could easily have given in right then. She could open up to Quincy. Wrap her arms around her. Fall back into the bed together.

But she scooped her inner strength off the bottom of

the lake of lust. Giving in right now would not serve her. She needed to be on equal footing with Quincy. And this wasn't going to cut it.

Missy turned them both, pushing Quincy against the wall of the narrow hallway. Quincy let out a low moan. Missy moved back, breaking the kiss. She pulled away from Quincy's arms. Now she was taking up the walkway in the hall, Quincy up against the wall staring at her with lust-wrecked eyes.

"We can talk when I get back." Missy didn't wait for a response. She turned on her heel and walked right out the door.

****

Penny was an excellent dinner date. Perhaps it was because she was a nurse that she was capable of completely figuring out and delivering what Missy needed at that moment. Bottomless glasses of red wine and conversation that had nothing to do with their spouses was on the menu alongside decadent appetizers and rich desserts.

Missy could almost forget the expression on Quincy's face when she left her standing in the hallway of the bungalow. Almost.

And as the evening wound down, Missy knew she would have to confront that again. Either that or another lonely night. She knew which was worse. She dreaded Quincy's absence far more than she did the hard conversation that was to come. And maybe that's why she ordered a second bottle of wine and sipped it slowly while chatting with Penny. But as the bottle emptied, her fate drew nearer. And eventually, she couldn't stop herself from voicing it aloud.

"Quincy and I are in a fake marriage."

Penny's face appropriately reflected the normal amount of shock at such a statement. "Okay. Wow. Um. Why?"

"She wanted to do it for a number of reasons, a lot of which have to do with her being kind of famous. She's a dog trainer on T.V."

"Yeah. I know. I've seen the show. But I didn't want to say anything."

Missy took a sip of wine. "So, yeah. She had reasons." She didn't even want to think about the complications with Quincy's ex, so she didn't mention those.

"And what about you?"

"What about me?"

"Why did you enter into a fake marriage?"

"I wanted to escape my life and start over. This felt like a good way to do that, if a little extreme." Having confessed her deep, dark secret to a stranger over dinner in a remote national park in the middle of the jungle made her suddenly light-headed.

Penny took a delicate sip of wine and narrowed her eyes as if she were working out a complex math problem in her head. "I see."

"Is that your only reaction?"

Penny chuckled. "No. But I didn't think you'd want to hear that your love life sounds like the plot of a romance novel."

"Actually, I'd be okay with that. Because then I'd be guaranteed a happy ending."

Penny laughed and pointed her finger at Missy. "That's true. Here." She tipped the bottle over Missy's glass. "Let's think about that over some more wine."

Chapter 10

Be Honest About Your Hang-Ups

Quincy stared at the closed door. She'd become used to being the one to leave in her life. She'd been the one to keep the distance between her and her brothers after their parents' death. She'd been the one to leave her exes. Hell, Quincy had left the entire mainland of the United States.

Now she stood alone, and swamped with a confusing combination of guilt, hurt, and raging jealousy. It tangled up her mind and her body. She was unsure if she should wait in the room, go for a run to sort out her thoughts, or go find Missy and see exactly who she was meeting.

The latter idea was extremely tempting. Rarely in her life had Quincy felt the flame of jealousy burn so hot in her gut as it had tonight. But there was no denying that something baser had inhabited her brain and her heart.

Her heart. What a stupid thought. Missy was a gorgeous acquaintance, a friend even; one she desired physically in ways she'd barely ever experienced. It could very well be a product of her age. She'd heard a lot of things about the increased libido of a woman in her mid-to-late thirties. Surely what she felt for Missy had more to do with the sweet smile and incredible figure than some deep-seated feelings.

She dropped down on the end of the bed. There would be no running after her bride. As soon as the image of herself hiding behind a potted plant, spying on Missy and her date entered her mind, she filled with shame. No, Quincy would wait right here and figure out exactly what she needed to say to set things back to where they had been before last night. Maybe even put them in a better place.

****

It took three long hours before the door rattled. Quincy sat up, pulling the phone away from her ear. "Olivia, I gotta go. She's back."

"Okay. Remember, don't be an asshole."

"Thanks. Love you." She turned off the phone and threw it onto the nightstand.

Missy stepped through the doorway. She looked exactly the same as when she left except that her lipstick had been replaced by the stain of red wine and little wisps of hair that had been tamed earlier now flitted around her head.

She dropped the keycard on the counter of the kitchenette and marched to the center of the room. She slammed her hands on her hips and looked down at Quincy. "Okay. Let's talk. On the beach." She stuck her thumb behind her toward the door.

Quincy jumped up. "Okay."

As she followed Missy through the bungalow, she slipped on her thong sandals. She barely made it through the door as it swung shut in Missy's wake. But Quincy managed to keep up as Missy wove a path through the other round, squat bungalows to the wide-open beach.

It wasn't until they reached the water's edge, Quincy walking beside Missy under the clear moonlight, that Missy finally spoke. "Here's the deal, if you want to hear it." She glanced sideways at Quincy, who nodded quickly. "I thought I was Ace for a long time. I would date people, but when we would kiss or try to get intimate, I just didn't feel anything. I thought they were objectively attractive, but I didn't feel anything. You know what I mean?"

"I've read about it. But I would be lying if I said I understood it from personal experience. I've always been attracted to women sexually regardless of their personality." She chuckled, thinking of Gina. "Sometimes in spite of it."

"All my friends were the same way. So, I joined a local group for asexual and aromantic people to try to figure myself out. Then I had a girlfriend in college, and everything changed."

"Sparks?"

"So many sparks."

"So you figured out you're demisexual."

"Yes. And I should have told you before last night. My attraction to you has been growing slowly over time."

Quincy's footsteps faltered. The message was clear. For Missy, growing attraction equaled growing feelings. "Okay. So what do you want to do with that?"

"First off, I thought you should know."

"Thank you for telling me. And I'm sorry I didn't react the way I should have last night. I'm glad you told me, and I want you to know that I will do what I can to fulfill your needs in this marriage."

Missy stopped walking and turned to Quincy. Her brow scrunched up. "That sounds so clinical."

"Sorry. I guess so. Let me try that again. Do you want to have sex with me?"

"Oh, hell yeah. But there's something else you should know. I have a hard time having an orgasm."

Every nerve in Quincy's body sparked. She was a

sexual being to her core. And if anything was going to push her over the hump of misgivings around having a sexual relationship with Missy, it was this.

"I'm sorry. What?"

Missy dipped her head. Her voice, soft and barely audible, she said, "I haven't had too many. From other people. Or like, any."

Quincy shivered. She loved a challenge. Thrived on them. It's why she'd chosen to train dogs. The more difficult the dog's issues, the more excited she was to tackle them.

As much as this challenge might be the most riveting one she'd ever faced, she wasn't completely ruled by her libido. There was still the major problem of Missy's feelings, which were already there, already developed. That ship had left the dock, and one way or another, Quincy would have to navigate that.

Why not give Missy some great experiences in the meantime?

"We should start walking back," she said, as casually as she could manage. Then, because she couldn't hold it in, she added. "I need to fix this right now."

To her surprise Missy laughed. The sound, soft and perfect, ran straight up Quincy's spine. "We can, but there's more to talk about."

Quincy turned around, placing a hand on the small of Missy's back and guiding her back toward the bungalow. "Yes. I need to tell how sorry I am that I was such an ass last night so you can fully forgive me."

Missy smiled at her. Now that they were walking back toward the lodge, her face was lit up from the front, and it was gorgeous. "I forgive you. I wanted to talk about your family. I get the distinct impression that they don't know we're married. And I want to talk about that."

The abrupt change in subject was jarring. But Quincy was willing to go along with it. "Actually, Olivia says they found out through social media."

"So, you didn't tell them?"

"No. I didn't."

"Is it because you're ashamed of me?"

Quincy stopped and took Missy by both shoulders. She turned her so they were face to face. "Oh my god, no. Why would you think that?"

"Why wouldn't I? Why else would you keep it a secret from them while telling the rest of the world?"

"No. It has nothing to do with you. I swear. It's about me and them. We have issues."

"What kind of issues?"

In less than sixty seconds, Quincy had gone from wanting to rush Missy back to their bungalow for a long, slow session of incredible sex to talking about the most painful thing in her life. The pivot had her reeling. But she took a deep breath and prepared to barrel forward. Just then, her phone rang. Gina's ring. She rolled her eyes, hit the reject button, and turned back to Missy.

"My parents died in a car crash eight years ago. My brothers and my sister-in-law and I all had to deal with the fallout. They wanted to do that by constantly talking and grieving together. I wanted to be alone with it. Eventually, the difference in how we handled it led to two camps, them and me. So they're super close, and I'm the outsider, a condition of my own making."

Quincy ran a hand through her hair. Talking about her parents' death was easier these days. But the way she'd pushed away her remaining family was harder. "They walk on eggshells around me. They want to throw their arms around me and squeeze; that's how they are with each other. But I won't let them, so they tread carefully. I have talked to them since the wedding. But we didn't talk about our marriage. I figured they would find out eventually and bring it up, but they never did."

"Because they're walking on eggshells around you?"

"Yeah. And I'm apparently not brave enough to bring it up myself."

"Why would telling them we are married require bravery?"

It was a fair question. But the answer tasted like chalk on her tongue as it spilled out. "Because that would mean letting them in, and I'm terrified of letting anyone in."

Missy moved before Quincy realized what was happening. She wrapped Quincy in her arms, drawing her body into her own. Quincy's head rested against Missy's. This spot felt so warm and safe that Quincy couldn't stop the single tear that dripped from her right eye.

Missy's hand moved gently over Quincy's back. "What do you want to do about that?"

The question nearly broke Quincy. But she couldn't let it. She'd bent far enough. She wouldn't go any further today. "Right now, I'd like to be alone with you."

Missy took Quincy's hand, and they made their way through the dark toward the bungalow. Quincy penetrated the silence with one statement, alone and out of context. "I just don't know how to close that gap."

But Missy seemed to understand. "Maybe we could start by having a conversation with your family about the marriage, like we did with my parents. We could do it together." She squeezed Quincy's hand.

Quincy picked up their pace, stepping onto the stone path that wove through the bungalows toward theirs. In a few moments they would be in the sanctuary of their room, where being laid bare would be so much more intimate.

"We could do that. Maybe tomorrow."

When they reached their room, Missy moved ahead of Quincy and opened the door, then stood to the side and gestured for Quincy to enter. When they were both nestled inside, just the glow of a dim light near the bed guiding their way, Missy shut the door. Neither of them moved to hit the switch that would bathe them in harsh, artificial light. Instead, they remained in the shadows.

Quincy's shoulders relaxed, an ache accompanying the action and reflecting how tense she'd been for the last few hours. Missy passed Quincy in the hallway, making her way into the main room. She stood at the foot of the bed and turned to face her wife.

"Thank you for telling me all of that."

"Thanks for putting up with all my shit."

Missy smiled. She was beautiful standing there. Quincy couldn't help but take a step toward her. Missy held out her hands, and Quincy took them in her own.

"So, I guess what we've learned tonight is that I'm insecure about my sexual experience, and you have a big wall you've built around you."

Quincy tugged on Missy's hands, bringing them closer together. The hem of Missy's dress brushed against Quincy's thighs just below her shorts. "Sounds about right. I also learned that I'm capable of irrational jealousy."

Missy tipped her head. "Really? I mean. I wasn't sure if you were really jealous of my dinner with Penny, or just being…"

"A controlling ass?"

Missy flashed a contrite smile and nodded.

"So jealous." Quincy wrapped her arm around Missy's lower back, bringing her body flush against Quincy's. "Who is this Penny person anyway?"

"The redhead we met on the beach with her wife." Missy raised her hand and stroked Quincy's cheek. "Nothing to be jealous of. The only person I'm interested in having anything more than conversation with is right here, right now."

Quincy leaned down and kissed her bride.

Chapter 11

Good Things Come to Those Who Wait

Fire ignited in Missy's lips and spread down quickly as Quincy kissed her with rich, unencumbered passion. The wake of warmth that followed Quincy's fingers as they trailed slowly up Missy's back and over to her ribs, then down again across her side, burned in the most delicious way. The feel of her palm spreading across Missy's right hip, her grip needy, swelled in Missy's heart until she feared it might burst.

Their bodies pressed together. Missy's legs were just far enough apart for Quincy's right thigh to fit perfectly into the space. Her breasts fit like puzzle pieces just below Quincy's. Quincy curved over, leaning down to lock their lips in a chaotic dance of want and need.

Missy was only a passive recipient for the briefest moment. Then her limbs were energized by the sparks racing through her. She wanted to be touched, kissed, pushed to the brink. But she also wanted to do the same to the object of her desire.

Moving her hand up to Quincy's hair, she wound her fingers into the short locks and pulled her head down, pressing Quincy further into her. Quincy moaned, sending Missy into the most pleasant spiral of sensation she'd ever experienced.

Motivated by that sexy sound, she moved her hands to Quincy's ribs and pushed her. Quincy followed her direction, stepping backward toward the bed. Quincy whirled Missy around, reversing their positions so that the back of Missy's knees were pressed against the mattress. Then Quincy dropped her onto the bed, followed her down. She caught Missy's fall with one hand bracing Missy's back and the other holding her own weight above Missy.

With Quincy hovering above her, Missy let out her own low moan. She ran her hand down Quincy's side and over onto her hard runner's ass. Quincy pressed her hips into Missy. Quincy's mouth then trailed down her neck, then over her clavicle, down into the "V" created by the flowery dress.

"Quincy," Missy whispered.

Quincy lifted her head. Bright eyes stared back at her, pupils like disks. Her flushed cheek was warm under Missy's fingers as she brushed it gently. "Take this dress off me. Please."

Quincy pressed a kiss right in the deepest part of the dress, then she pulled herself up so they were face-to-face. "No."

The word shocked Missy out of her languid mood like a rubber band snapping on her wrist. "What?"

Quincy dropped a soft kiss on Missy's lips and stroked her neck with gentle fingers. "I have a better idea."

Her alarm faded. Whatever sensual thing Quincy had in mind, she was game. And the wicked look on Quincy's face let her know she wouldn't regret going along with it.

"I think we should agree, up front, that we aren't going to have sex tonight."

Every bit of concern over this situation flooded back into Missy. Was this going to be a repeat of last night? "I don't understand."

"Here's the thing." Quincy propped herself up on one

elbow while her other hand traced slow circles on the side of Missy's neck. "I don't want you to feel any pressure."

Missy panicked. Would her hang up cause her to lose out on the most sensual experience of her life so far? "I don't. I swear."

Quincy dropped another reassuring kiss on her lips. "I refuse. Refuse, to allow you to have another sexual experience that doesn't end in at least one really great orgasm. One is not nearly enough, frankly, but I'm willing to set a low bar with the intention of blowing it out of the water."

Missy didn't know whether to laugh or cry. The sound that came out of her was a strange mixture of the two.

"So." Quincy took a lock of Missy's hair between her finger and thumb. She pulled gently, smoothing out the spiral curl, then released it, watching it bounce back and land against Missy's neck. "I need you to be completely comfortable."

"I mean, I'm comfortable right now."

"Oh, I can tell. And I want to keep that comfort. And that confidence." She pressed her thigh into Missy.

Missy threw her head back and moaned, loud and clear this time.

"Oh, yeah. You know how sexy you are."

A new picture of herself formed in Missy's mind. And she liked it.

"I don't want to lose that to your head." Quincy tapped Missy's temple. "If you start thinking about sex, you could spiral. Then you'll tense up. In fact, your body did just that right before you asked me to take off your clothes. I felt it."

Missy bit her lip. Something about the way Quincy paid attention to her body with such intimate focus was so very hot. She squirmed a little, the movement bringing her into more contact with Quincy's thigh and nearly causing another display of need. But she wouldn't be embarrassed by it, any of it.

"Okay. But can we keep making out?"

Quincy's words were soft but fierce. "Fuck yes." Then she pressed her lips back to Missy's, and she was lost again.

****

Missy was glad she'd talked Quincy into having dinner with Penny and her wife Linda. As much they'd been lost in one another for the past seventy-two hours, a little company couldn't hurt. It would help them readjust to having to act normal in the presence of others when they headed back to St. Croix in just two days—a thought that plagued Missy in every moment she wasn't reveling in Quincy's touch.

Linda, who turned out to be the most extroverted of the bunch, poured more wine into Quincy's glass. "L.A., San Francisco, and San Diego, and here we meet in Venezuela. Who saw that coming?" She emptied the bottle into her own glass and raised it. "To Californian's meeting a continent away!"

They all participated in the toast and drank. The server came by with the appetizers and asked if they wanted another bottle. "Absolutely," Linda said.

"What is it you do, Linda?" Quincy asked. "Because whatever it is, I feel like you should have my job."

Linda laughed. "I'm sure I would enjoy training dogs—not that I have a clue how to. But I could never be on T.V."

"What?" Quincy lifted one hand, and owing to how close they were pressed together on their side of the table, it brushed against Missy. "You are perfect for television."

Missy and Quincy didn't have to sit so close that Missy was practically in her wife's lap. There was plenty of room around the table. But it was like that now. They wound around one another, were drawn to each other's physical space like a pair of planets in a double orbital system.

Linda waved a hand at Quincy. "You might think, but I have terrible stage fright."

"It's true," Penny said. "The company once asked her to do a YouTube video for their channel, and she completely froze."

"I'll stick to what I do best, numbers. No cameras for me, thanks." She glanced at Penny, eyes sparkling. "I'm not good looking enough for cameras, anyway. Not like my gorgeous wife."

Penny blushed and leaned over to reward Linda with a kiss on the cheek. Missy watched without the usual awkwardness of a single person sitting with a loving couple or a person in a new relationship, unsure of where they stand, uncomfortable with the juxtaposition of the display across from them.

No, she didn't have that familiar feeling creeping up in her gut. No need to put on an act across the table that she was fine with being the third wheel or that she, too, could kiss and coddle her date. Her physical being, in such close proximity to Quincy, had never been so at ease.

She hadn't spent a lot of time analyzing it over the past three days. But as she sat back in her chair, one hand resting lazily on Quincy's thigh, watching as her wife and their new friends ate the oysters her vegetarian soul had no desire for, her mind meandered.

She and Quincy had broken the seal on their sexual tension that night after the walk on the beach. Quincy jumped over the hurdle that had been keeping her from touching Missy. She'd also calmed Missy's insecurities by changing the expectations.

And those expectations held. Lots of kissing, constant touching, and tons of heavy petting. But no sex. And with each touch, kiss, or nuzzle, the tension ratcheted up. After all those hours of close proximity, Missy's body swam in a constant low-level buzz. It was not at all unpleasant. She'd come to enjoy it. At the same time, she desperately wanted it to explode into a supernova.

Missy tried to school her features, sure a dopey smile was pasted on her face. She peeked over at Quincy who was caught up in conversation with Linda. They were discussing something about television, though she'd lost track of exactly what. It didn't matter. Quincy's animated expression, her flailing hands and wide eyes, were all fodder for Missy's sappy smiles.

In the time they'd known each other, Quincy hadn't been exuberant like this, but something had snapped inside her over the past couple of days. She hiked with her gaze up, rather than pointed down at her feet. She kept her head on a swivel, constantly taking in the sights and sounds. Her finger must be nearly worn out for all the things she'd pointed out to Missy on their journeys. And at night, she was warm, open, and incredibly sexy. The care she took with Missy only increased Missy's need for her.

Independence had always been at the core of Missy's personality. She suspected Quincy—no she knew—Quincy was the same way. She'd admitted as much to Missy the other night. And yet, these two people, each an island unto themselves, were drawn easily into each other's circle.

"What do you think Missy?"

Quincy's words snapped her out of her quiet contemplation. She sat up in the mildly uncomfortable wooden chair. "Um, what?"

Quincy placed her hand over the one Missy still had on Quincy's knee and squeezed it. "Did we lose you for a minute there?"

"Afraid so. What did I miss?"

"We were thinking of taking a dip after dinner in that swimming hole on the other side of the resort. Linda said that when they went there around this time on Wednesday, it was deserted."

"Oh yeah. That sounds great." She flipped her hand over and interlaced her fingers with Quincy's. "I'm game."

Penny leaned forward, her forearms resting on the table. "I have to say, you two look like a real couple to me."

"Penny!" Linda turned on her wife.

"What?" Penny gestured toward Missy and Quincy. "They said they had a marriage of convenience."

Missy was too caught up in the warmth of the words "like a real couple" to figure out how to respond. But Quincy must have been on a different plane of existence. She laughed, a sparkle in her eye as she pinned her gaze to Penny.

"You know I've been thinking about that lately. What will we look like to the outside world when we get back home?"

Wait. What? While she'd been reveling in sweet glances and soft touches, Quincy had been calculating their appearance?

While Missy couldn't find it in herself to ask that question right now, Penny did it for her. She leaned over the table, bringing her face as close to Quincy as possible, eyes narrowed, brow furrowed. "So, what's the goal then? To make people believe it?"

The sparkle never left Quincy's eye. Nor did her face fall at the challenge Penny presented. "All the people that know us personally know that we got married for reasons other than the usual. And social media." She shrugged. "Well, that's just social media. Putting our marriage out there is just convenient." She chuckled at her own joke.

But the pun wasn't worthy of a laugh. What had been a business deal two weeks ago was something else now.

Penny leaned back. "So, it's not for show?"

Quincy shrugged. "Yes and no."

Two opposite sides of one coin. Both with serious implications to Missy's heart.

"Okay, let's say a reporter asked you about the marriage? What would you say?"

"I'm not that famous. Just barely famous enough for strangers to follow me on social media. That's all."

Penny waved her hand at Quincy. "I know you've done interviews, Quincy. I've seen them. Come on. What would you say?"

Linda placed a hand on Penny's elbow. "You're very pushy tonight."

"I'm looking out for my friends. I just want to help."

Quincy smiled. "It's okay. It's actually good to talk through all this before we get back. We really haven't done that. My agent wants to talk about it all the time, but I can't stand discussing anything with her. She's a real pain in the ass." She shrugged. "But she's my mom's god daughter, so what're you gonna do. Anyway, I'm definitely not interested in talking to Myra about this."

"So," Penny pressed. "A reporter asks point blank, 'I heard this was a fake marriage.' What do you say?"

"I know what I would say." Quincy turned her head.

"What would you say, Missy?"

Jolted, Missy scrambled, sitting up straighter in her chair. To stall, she took a sip of wine. Flutters of anxiety rose in her chest. She didn't want to think about reporters. "I don't know. I want to hear your answer, first."

"Sure. I'd say: It's not fake at all. It's a real marriage, just like anyone else's. And just like with straight couples, gay couples have myriad reasons for getting married. All of them valid. All of them personal."

Their marriage was personal now. And just like everything else in Missy's life that she coveted as private, it was fodder for other people's speculation. She thought she could handle that when they were talking about it in the abstract, and when it was truly a fake marriage. But now her relationship with Quincy was as real as the waves lapping on the shore of the lagoon, as the ground beneath her feet, as Quincy's hand in hers.

"And that's it?" Penny pressed. "You're not going to tell us what your reasons are?"

Linda groaned. But Quincy just grinned wider. "Nope. I'm not."

Penny clapped her hands. "Well done! You're ready."

Maybe Quincy was ready, but Missy wasn't.

Chapter 12

Try to Prevent Conflict with Your Fake Spouse

"I got a whole pitcher from the bar." Quincy carefully placed the tray on the glass table that sat between the two lounge chairs. She dropped into her own chair before lifting one of the margarita glasses toward her wife.

Missy stared out at the setting sun. Quincy stayed frozen for a moment, hand in mid-air with a glass perched in it, condensation dripping onto her wrist. The scene—splattered with reddish-orange hues painting the sky above the shadowed tepui in the distance—was almost as beautiful as the woman beside her.

For two days, Missy had been distant, lost in her own thoughts. Every time Quincy had tried to engage her in conversation, Missy responses were short and vague. And the intimacy they'd cultivated seemed to have died on the vine.

She'd already cooked Missy special meals in the kitchenette, planned a hike complete with a picnic, and tried to get Missy to go to the waterfall with her. But nothing was working. Missy was upset about something that happened during the dinner with Penny and Linda. But Quincy had no idea what she'd done wrong.

Now, on the last night of their honeymoon, Quincy would try anything to break the spell. Tonight's plan was to start them off the way Missy had started off the entire trip, with margaritas on the private patio of their bungalow. The details about where to go if that didn't work were still being formed in her mind, but surely the alcohol would help point to a solution.

Her arm was starting to ache. But before she could open her mouth to remind Missy that she was sitting there with a drink, Missy swooped the glass out of her hand.

"Thank you. Sorry."

"I thought we would end the trip the way we started it."

No answer. Nothing.

"Except it isn't quite the same. I feel like things are very different between us now."

Missy spun her head to the side and finally looked at Quincy. "I'm sorry. I've been in my head lately."

"You wanna talk about it?"

Missy let out a massive sigh. "I wanted to have formulated a solution first, then talk about it. But I just keep going around in circles, and I'm not getting anywhere."

Quincy sat on the edge of her lounge chair facing Missy. That Missy was spread out, perpendicular to her wasn't ideal, but at least she'd turned her head to face Quincy.

Quincy spun her margarita glass in her hands slowly, the action keeping her from reaching out to touch Missy the way she wanted to. "Why don't you run it by me, and we'll see if we can find a solution together."

Missy took a sip of her drink, then stared out at the scenery again. Quincy really wished she'd look at her. "It's the whole press thing. I know this sounds stupid because I knowingly entered a marriage of convenience with someone who has a freaking television show. So I should have known better. If I wanted to stay out of the spotlight, why did I take a job on a T.V. show, then marry its star? So stupid." She turned to peer at Quincy, her rich, brown eyes wide.

"Okay back up. Because I don't think you regret getting married, right?"

"No. That's not it." Missy sat up and swung her legs around so she was sitting on the edge of her chair, mirroring Quincy. She placed her drink on the ground beside her chair. "It's more that I had a really hard time with the local press and social media gossip scene when I was younger, and I tried to avoid being in the spotlight. And now I put myself there, and I feel pretty stupid about having done that. I should have known it would give me this ache." She placed her hands over her stomach.

Quincy dropped her own hands on Missy's knees. "Tell me about this ache."

"It's situational anxiety. That's what my therapist said. I took meds for it for a while. But then I stopped a few years back. The thing is, it was never that bad what they wrote about me…it was just stupid stuff. I just didn't like seeing myself online, in the images. It made me sweat. My stomach hurt. I was always terrified to read the caption that went with it. I never read the comments. Thank god. I just wanted to be anonymous. Eventually, after college, the press kind of forgot about me. There was one story about me becoming a dog trainer, but apparently that was too boring, and I haven't come up again in almost a year. And now." She tossed her hands in the air. "I was so casual about it when we were talking about getting married, but it really came down on me the other night at dinner."

"What was it about that conversation that made it come to the surface like this?"

Missy pulled her hands away from her stomach and placed them over Quincy's. "That's one of the things I've been running around in my head. All I've come up with is that the idea of people talking about our marriage when it was totally fake was one thing…"

"But now it's different?"

Missy shrugged, but her eyes were pleading.

Quincy took in a deep breath. Missy's feelings were still something that made her uneasy. She didn't want to hurt Missy, and at this point that seemed inevitable. But she could be there for her now. She could give her everything she had while their marriage lasted. "Okay. So tell me what would make you feel better?"

Missy let out a small, sad laugh. "I've been running that over in my head, too. I'm frustrated that I'm wasting our time in this beautiful place, alone together, thinking about what might happen when we get back to the island."

"So, I'm hearing that the best thing to do right now is take your mind off it?" Quincy let the fingers on her right hand move higher up Missy's thigh, sliding over her soft skin.

Missy leaned forward, bringing her lips within inches of Quincy's. She hovered there, their noses just barely brushing. "That's an excellent idea."

"Yeah?" Quincy tipped her head and touched Missy's lips with her own, just a tiny touch, a breath, a whisper. "I think that's something I can do."

Missy moved forward, sliding her legs over Quincy's so she straddled her lap. She took Quincy's face in her hands and consumed her mouth.

Two days without this intimacy accentuated how essential it was to Quincy's being. The careful control Quincy had tried so hard to maintain over emotion and passion snapped in that moment. Broken completely. Shattered beyond repair.

She stood up, taking Missy with her. Not once did their lips separate. She carried her into the bungalow, stopping for just a moment so Missy could close the door to the patio. They landed on the bed, as they'd done a few times before. Only Quincy didn't school her hands this time. She tugged at Missy's cotton t-shirt until she managed to get it off. In the brief moment their lips were separated, Missy did the same to her.

Then they dove back in, unwilling to spend any time apart. Missy pushed, and Quincy obliged, rolling so the smaller woman could lay over her. The skin of their stomachs touching, the cotton of Quincy's sports bra pressed against the lace of Missy's push-up. Bare legs tangled below their shorts.

Quincy needed to touch Missy. If she didn't, she might die right here like this. But even as her hand skimmed along soft, smooth skin she knew she needed to make sure Missy was okay. Because as much as desire ruled her brain, there was something even greater standing in its shadow, something she couldn't name.

Quincy pulled her lips away and placed them beside the gentle curve of Missy's ear. "May I?" There was no need to explain further. The tips of her fingers caressed the thin elastic band at the top of Missy's panties.

"Oh my god, please." Missy's breathy plea nearly toppled Quincy over the edge.

The next few minutes were magical. Quincy soared. She was trapped in a place she never wanted to leave, pillowed in the most amazing sensations as she moved her fingers with grace and precision while keeping watch on every movement. Missy's lips caught between her teeth as she strained to keep in a moan. Her chest expanded and deflated as her breaths came quick and rough. The pulse in Missy's neck beat as blood coursed through her, and when Quincy leaned down and suckled one nipple, a low groan emitted from that perfect, arched throat.

Missy's body quivered, and Quincy knew she was close. She almost wanted to slow down the moment, to draw out this essential first for her wife.

Missy opened her eyes, and Quincy held her gaze as she carefully orchestrated the crescendo building inside Missy. Her pants and short moans turned into a long keening sound as her quivering body ramped up to full vibration.

Every part of her was affected as the orgasm washed over her body. Her unarticulated shout turned to a repetition of Quincy's name as she slowly came down off the perch of ecstasy.

In that moment, something shifted, and Quincy knew that she would never be the same.

****

Daylight hit Quincy's eyes. Missy lay beside her. Smooth skin glinted in the muted sunlight cast through the bungalow's window.

Everything changed last night. In this cozy bungalow oasis, it was easy to accept that the moments of intimacy had forever altered her essential make up. But what would happen when they returned to the island? She had veered off course, and now she needed to make a new plan. This time, Missy's wants and needs would take precedence over her own.

As the slice of sunlight on the ceiling grew into a fat stripe, Missy's warm body moved. She reached one arm out, stretching toward the headboard.

Quincy shifted to her side to get a better view of her waking wife. Just then, the trill sound of Gina calling emitted from her phone's perch on the nightstand. Quincy hit the reject button and turned back to Missy.

"Hey."

Missy's sweet smile nearly melted Quincy's heart. "Who knew the last night of the honeymoon would be the best?"

"It definitely was."

"Wish we weren't going home today."

"Me, too."

Missy propped herself up on her elbow. "Should we, like, discuss going home?"

Quincy dropped a kiss on Missy's soft mouth. "I was just thinking about that. But I wished I wasn't. There are so many better things to discuss." She ran her hand down Missy's side. "Like if you're ticklish or not. And if so, where?"

Missy squirmed away from her touch, but then immediately pressed herself back against Quincy's side. "I would stay here forever if we could, but we can't. And we need to figure out what we're going to tell people about us when we go home."

"I don't want to say what I think," Quincy said. What if Missy disagreed and shut her out again? She couldn't afford to have that happen. She was desperate to hang onto this new reality.

Missy ran a finger along Quincy's cheek. "Why not?"

"I don't want to say the wrong thing."

Missy scrunched up her brow. "Am I so unreasonable?"

"No." Quincy kissed the tip of her nose. "You're beautiful, and I don't want you to leave my bed."

Missy harrumphed. "Well, I'll tell you what I think we should do."

"Okay. Lay it on me."

"I think it's best if what we have now stays between us."

Quincy tried to keep the breath she released from being too obvious. But she was pretty sure she failed. "Yeah. I think it can be just our thing for now."

"Our thing. I like the sound of that."

"Me, too."

With that settled, Quincy leaned in, intent on starting something in the early morning light, something sexy that would lead to Missy crying out in ecstasy and Quincy smirking in satisfied delight.

But Missy moved her head back and put up a hand. "Wait. There's more."

Quincy tried to prevent a frown, but based on Missy's chuckle, she hadn't succeeded. "Oh my god. Don't pout."

"Sorry. I just really wanted to make love now. Can we just skip to that?"

Missy laughed again. Quincy usually hated the idea of being the butt of anyone's joke, but the way Missy lit up when she was amused might be the best thing ever. Also, Missy's thighs were pressed against her own and the way they shook with her laughter created a desire she could barely control.

She dropped a kiss on Missy's neck. "Please, can this be a short conversation?"

"Once you fall off of the celibacy wagon you don't get back on, do you?"

"Not with you naked in my bed."

"That's actually what I wanted to talk to you about."

Quincy ripped her lips away from the delicate skin at the base of Missy's throat and stared into those dark brown eyes. She couldn't be putting the brakes on this, could she?

"I want to…" Missy bit her lip. Her right incisor was

just slightly offset from her left, and it was so stinking cute Quincy wanted to lick it.

"You want what, baby? Whatever it is, I'll do it." Gladly. Happily.

"That's just it. It's what I want to do."

"Okay. What?"

Missy pushed her hips into Quincy's. Quincy gave way and rolled onto her back. She helped Missy crawl on top of her, placing her palms on Missy's hips.

Missy bit her lip again. Her eyes were bright, but guarded.

"Seriously, baby. You're killing me. I swear, whatever it is, I'm in. Kink, toys, whatever. You want me to wear a strap-on? I don't have one here, but when we get back to the island—"

Missy put her hand over Quincy's mouth. "I mean. All that is cool, too. But what I really want right now is…"

"Yes?"

"I want to go down on you."

"Oh my god. Yes. Yes. I mean. Is there a no to that? I mean. Yes. Can you? Please. Jesus. Now I can't stop talking." The last word escaped her mouth as Missy trailed kisses over her stomach.

She paused for just the briefest, most delicious of moments, then she licked a path across Quincy's clit with voracious zeal. And that's when the obscenities really flew from Quincy's mouth.

****

First class was a luxury Quincy never wasted. She didn't grow up as a first-class person, and she wouldn't have flown first class on her own dime for a relatively short flight. But Missy booked this flight, and she did grow up in first class.

Quincy was grateful. A row of two, just her and Missy. Lots of leg room. Hand holding on the armrest between them. Free mimosas. It was the best way to travel, especially when she was headed back to a reality she wasn't at all ready for.

She turned to ogle at her bride sitting in the window seat. Missy gazed out at the landing strip. Her perfect curls rested on her shoulder. Her dark brown lashes fluttered as she blinked against the bright sun streaming through the oval window. Quincy squeezed her hand.

Missy swiveled her head. "Are you ready to do this? Resume our regular lives?"

"No. Not at all."

Missy leaned over and gave Quincy a quick peck on the lips. "You'll be all right."

She would be, with this remarkable woman at her side.

The landing was smooth. The exit easy, since they were in the first row. Dropping into the Henry E. Rohlson Airport was as simple as could be. Even retrieving their luggage from the carrousel went well.

It was as they turned away, bags in hand, that it all went to hell. A gang of six people, all with phones held at the ready, swarmed them. One was a local television reporter, another a content creator Quincy had once done an interview with. The remaining four were strangers, but their demeanor and the way they pressed together and shouted questions made it clear they were also some sort of news reporters.

She'd gained some notoriety for the show, but it had never been worthy of this kind of ambush. Had something massive happened at the kennels while they were away? Had her ex made headlines with something stupid that was now leaking into her life?

Questions bombarded them from every angle: "Quincy! What's it like being married to an heiress of an iconic American brand? Did you have a honeymoon worthy of royalty? What does the Green family think of your running off to elope?"

Quincy glanced over at Missy. This was everything Missy had feared. Two days of worry over exactly this moment. Quincy had momentarily banished it from Missy's mind last night only to be hit full force in the face with it today.

Missy had turned a sickly color. They had to get out of here.

Quincy spotted a restroom ten yards away. Grasping Missy's hand, she tugged her toward the reprieve. Inside she found it scantily populated, but some of the hoard could conceivably follow them in here, so Quincy pulled Missy into an open stall. They were jammed in, standing on either side of the toilet, backs against the smooth metal walls, luggage smashed into the space under the door.

Missy's eyes were as wide as dinner plates. "What are we going to do?"

"I'll call Jack. He's probably circling to pick us up, maybe he can come in and, I don't know, escort us out or something." Quincy kept one hand in Missy's while using the other to pull up Jack's number. But before she could call him, the phone rang in her hand. Myra.

"Hello?"

"Hey, I just parked. The circle drive is a nightmare."

"You're here?"

"Yeah. Jack and I switched. I'm picking you up in my sweet ride. Be grateful."

"I thought you weren't supposed to be here until tomorrow."

Missy's brow furrowed. Quincy rolled her eyes and

mouthed, "Myra."

"I came early. Where are you?"

"Missy and I are hiding in the bathroom near baggage claim."

"Why?"

"There are reporters here."

"Paparazzi!" The excitement in Myra's voice was unmistakable. "You've made it, kid."

Quincy wanted to cuss Myra out. Missy's well-being was more important than any stupid publicity for the show. She took a breath and reminded herself that Myra had no idea about Missy's issues with the press. "Okay, well as happy as that might make you, we're a little stressed out here. We need help."

Missy stood next to the toilet paper dispenser with sheer terror painted on her face. Quincy would do anything to get rid of that look.

But Myra wasn't getting it. "You and Missy both have experience with this. What's the panic about?" She sounded weirdly out of breath.

"Listen, Myra, I don't have time to explain. We need help. Please."

"No problem. Hit the 'share my location' on your phone and I'll be right there."

Myra hung up and Quincy held her phone out to Missy. "Share location?"

Missy took the phone and hit a few buttons on the screen before handing it back. "All set."

"I knew it was handy marrying a Gen Z-er."

"Didn't realize I was marrying a Millennial that has a Gen X relationship to technology."

This easy banter seemed to relax Missy, and Quincy was willing to chase it. "My brother got an Atari at an auction once. He has this thing for collecting old technologies. We all played it, and I kicked ass. So maybe there's something to that."

Finally, Missy smiled. Quincy sighed. Thank god. She leaned in, unable to stop herself from dropping a tender kiss on Missy's lips. But her leg running into the toilet kept her from anything more.

"Ugh. I hope we can escape the bathroom soon."

Missy's eyes grew wide again. "I'm sorry. My reaction is overblown."

Quincy kissed her cheek and squeezed her hand. "No. It's not. You have every right to not want to do this. Luckily Myra is here, and she's going to help."

"Why is she here a day early?"

"I have no idea." But a sneaking suspicion told Quincy it couldn't be good.

"I didn't tell you about how the press was when I came out."

"No. I guess not." Quincy's stomach clenched at the thought of Missy, young and vulnerable, coming out in an environment where her every move was scrutinized.

"It's San Francisco, so the LGBTQ influencers loved it. I got asked to all kinds of events. It felt good. I had a supportive community for a hot minute. But the other side of the coin was that the mainstream press pretended to think it was great while trying to find any reason to besmirch me. Especially since I was the second queer person in our famous family. They would show up at parties I was at and try to take pictures of me drunk. That kind of thing. In the end, it was a mixed bag. And if I hadn't already had the issues I told you about, it might not be so bad."

"But it was bad?"

"Yeah. God, I still feel so dumb for not thinking about this before."

A sharp pain struck Quincy in the chest. The idea that Missy might not have married her over this stung more than it should have. "Okay. Let's deal with that later, and focus on this moment, right now. Okay?"

Missy nodded. Then she flashed a sad smile. "Thank you, Quincy. For taking care of me."

Was she taking care of her? Quincy wasn't sure.

Missy clunked her knee on the toilet as she leaned over to give Quincy a kiss. This kiss wasn't so sweet and gentle either. Filled with passion and promise, Quincy might have gotten lost in it were it not for the banging on the stall door that jolted them both.

"Come on, ladies. Let's get this show on the road."

Chapter 13

Be Prepared to Explain Your Fake Marriage to Anyone and Everyone

After Myra dragged them out of the ladies' room, Missy silently followed along as they met head-to-head with the reporters and content creators who all stood waiting in a clump. Myra addressed them as if she were a queen, commanding that if they wanted to hear from Mrs. and Mrs. Adams, they would have to follow her.

The entire entourage wove through the airport like ducklings and headed out the front doors. The highlight of the entire ordeal, other than Quincy's kindness in the lavatory, was hearing herself be called Mrs. Adams repeatedly.

Myra came to a stop in a vacant area off to the side of the main airport drive. "Okay. Here's how this is going to go. You can use the pictures we take here, but only these. I better not see some picture of them walking into the bathroom or I will come after you. Understand?"

The reporters all nodded and mumbled, clearly as terrified of Myra as she wanted them to be. Missy stood hand in hand with Quincy behind Myra. When the camera clicks started emitting from the phones, Missy had to remind herself to smile. She hoped it didn't look too fake. But there was nothing to be done about that. This was awkward as hell.

"I have a question." A man in a pink polo shouted

toward them.

Why they had to shout when they were literally five feet away, Missy totally did not get. It's like reporters only knew how to shout. Like no one had ever taught them inside voices.

"Go ahead," Myra said.

"Why did you get married?"

Wow. Right to the hard stuff then.

Myra wasn't having it. "Why do people usually get married? Next."

Quincy touched Myra's arm. "No. We got this." She turned to Missy who nodded quickly. She had no idea what Quincy was going to say, but at this moment, she didn't have the energy to figure out what else they could possibly do. She was willing to let Quincy wing it. "We got married because we both needed something. What that was isn't any of your business. But we could help each other. And we like each other."

Warmth flowed through Missy, but a camera click threatened to wreck the moment. She shook it off, and squeezed Quincy's hand, wanting to hear what came next.

"And then." Quincy proceeded cautiously, her eyes examining Missy's. "We found out that we are a great team. And over the last two weeks our reasons changed."

More camera clicks. The dopey look on Missy's face would probably make for good clickbait.

"What about the original reasons. What did you need, Quincy? Money? Did you marry Missy for her family's money?"

The question was a slap in the face. Missy reeled back, then stepped forward. Her hand slipped away from Quincy as she approached the woman who'd asked. She was slightly taller than Missy, but only because she wore heels. Her hair was also brown and curly, but rather than ringlets cascading down her shoulders in a way that showed off the genes Missy inherited from her maternal grandmother, the reporter sported a bad perm.

Missy stepped to within a foot of the woman, staring straight into dull, mud-colored eyes. "I cannot believe you just asked that question. When in your life did someone tell you that it was okay to say something like that to someone?"

If the reporter was intimidated, she didn't let it show. She smirked. "So, is that a yes? Or a no?"

Behind her, Quincy called her name, but Missy ignored it. "How dare you!"

Myra dropped a hand on Missy's shoulder. When did she get so close? "There's a prenup, Kimber. You know that. Don't be an ass, or I'll make sure your half a million followers know about things you don't want them to know."

Missy wanted to wipe the smug look off Kimber's face. Instead, she allowed Myra to drag her back to her original spot, depositing her beside Quincy. Quincy scooped up her hand again and squeezed.

Missy was too angry to look over at her wife. It would temper some of the storm, and she wanted to hold onto it until this was over. Who knew what kind of asinine question was coming next?

"How was the honeymoon?"

Quincy answered that question, talking far longer than seemed necessary to expound on the beauty of the waterfalls and tepuis. She went into long, flowing descriptions of the serenity of the place, basically taking up time until they could say the entire interview session had lasted long enough.

"Missy!" A reporter spoke up the minute Quincy stopped to take a breath during a lengthy description of the lagoon at sunset. "Did you enjoy the time with your new wife? What was it like between you?"

"That's none of your business." Missy might have left it at that, but she didn't want the only recordings of her to be labeled by influencers as "the pissed off, spoiled heiress." She'd learned a lot from those years in the public eye. And if she didn't give them something else, she'd be a gif soon.

Impressed with the power surging through her in the face of these vultures—power she couldn't have begun to imagine would possess her when she was huddled in the bathroom stall minutes ago—she hitched up one side of her mouth. "But to tell the truth," Missy glanced over at Quincy now, letting the expression that she'd known would accompany that view take over her face, "it was a lot of fun." She turned back to the small crowd. "Everything a honeymoon should be."

It was the truth, and she was happy to leave it there. Apparently, so was Myra. She called the whole thing to an end and shooed the reporters out of the way as the three of them strolled off toward the parking lot.

The warmth of Quincy's palm buzzed through her as their hands came together while they walked. That simple action calmed her in a way nothing else could.

****

As soon as Missy's ass hit the leather seat in the back of Myra's car, Quincy hauled her across the space between them and captured her mouth in a rough, demanding kiss. When she pulled away, she whispered into Missy's ear. "That was so fucking hot, the way you stepped up to that reporter."

Missy reveled in both the image of her that Quincy had

painted and the way Quincy appreciated it. She might have shown her what it meant to her if Myra hadn't cleared her throat and started the engine.

"You did great, both of you. Also, are you planning to tell everyone about this?" Still looking ahead as she pulled out of the parking space, Myra spun her thumb to point at them.

"What's to tell?" Quincy asked.

Myra navigated her way through the dim parking garage and out into the bright daylight of a St. Croix afternoon. "Don't bullshit me. You two are sleeping together."

Quincy scoffed. "And what's wrong with that?"

Myra merged into traffic. "I didn't say anything was wrong with it. Far from it. It's about damn time you had a little fun. But what are you going to tell Jack and Henry? Or the rest of Missy's family. Or the crew."

Quincy gazed pointedly at Missy. "She means what do we tell all the people who know we have a marriage of convenience."

Missy sighed. "This," she pointed between them, "we agreed to keep a secret from the people who know us. But that feels like it will be hard."

"We don't have to decide right now." Quincy squeezed her hand and leaned back against the leather car seat.

She did have a point. Aside from her uncles and the film crew, it wasn't like they were going to see anyone in person anytime soon. And they could remain professional on set and play it by ear when they were in more casual settings. "True."

Missy spent the rest of the ride staring out the window while Myra and Quincy talked about what pictures and statements they would release on social media. She didn't care what image they portrayed publicly anymore. She just wanted to stay in this happy place with Quincy for as long as she could.

Without warning, Quincy shouted, "What the hell is going on?"

Missy jerked her head up and sharpened her gaze out the window. They were approaching the house, and packing their driveway was a fleet of rental cars. "Who's here?"

Myra turned to pull up into a space someone had purposely left open. "I might have neglected to tell you why I came to the island early." She threw the car into park and swiveled around in her seat to look at Quincy and Missy. "Missy's family is here."

"What?" Missy said. "What do you mean?"

"Your family. All of 'em. They want to throw you a real wedding."

"What?"

"Yep. Isn't that sweet? Also," Myra turned her gaze on Quincy, "they brought your family over, too." She grinned the most evil grin Missy had ever seen.

This time it was Quincy's turn to respond. But she didn't repeat Missy's question. All that came out of her mouth was, "Fuck!"

Chapter 14

Don't Involve Your Family in Your Fake Marriage

Quincy's quaint little cottage, her private space, her refuge, had been severely violated. The place was packed wall to wall with people. Both of her brothers, Brian and Karl, her sister-in-law, Keri, and her teenaged niece, Jordy, were draped about the furniture in the living room. They were joined by Missy's brother, Matt. Quincy and Missy managed to swing through with a "hey" and "talk to you in a minute" before being rushed into the kitchen where Missy's parents, Claire and Tom, her sister-in-law, Eliana, Jack, and Henry were waiting to bombard them.

Myra had better have a good life insurance plan, because Quincy was going to kill her.

"You don't have to worry about anything," Missy's mom, Claire, was saying. "We're making all the arrangements."

Missy, who had not once left Quincy's side from the moment they'd entered the lion's den, leaned over the counter toward her mother. "Mom, we didn't want a big wedding. That's why we did it the way we did."

"I know. And that's great. That's why this time we're going to do it our way, since it's for us." She patted Missy's cheek and turned her gaze to Quincy. "Quincy, dear, I didn't find out about your best friend, Olivia, until I got all your family here. But your sister-in-law called her, and she'll be getting on a plane in the morning in plenty of time for the wedding."

Olivia's presence might be the one bright spot in all of this.

"When, exactly, is this wedding going to occur?" Missy asked.

"On Saturday, honey. Then we'll leave on Sunday, and Jack says you pick up the filming for the show again on Monday. So, it will all work out perfectly." Claire clapped her hands together.

Except today was Thursday. Should Quincy be freaked out because the wedding was happening in two days or relieved that they'd all be gone in three?

"Where are you all staying?" The terror lying just beneath the surface of Missy's voice came through in her question.

Missy's father—Tom, he'd told Quincy to call him—patted Missy's hand. "It's all taken care of, sweetheart. We have a block of rooms at the resort just down the beach."

Words came out of Quincy's mouth without thought. "How did you do that?" It was impossible to get that many rooms on the island last minute.

Missy glanced at her and rolled her eyes. "Don't ask. He can get things done you wouldn't believe."

"But there is that Olivia problem," Claire said. "She doesn't have a room."

Quincy was about to say that it didn't matter. Olivia would stay at her place. Of course she would. She was the closest person to Quincy in the world. But she stopped herself. Something about throwing that out there seemed off.

Before she could fully examine the entire issue, Missy spoke. "Olivia can stay with us." She blinked up at Quincy, her expression uncertain.

Something struck Quincy in that moment. Something warm and complicated. “Yeah. Of course.”

“Great!” Claire clapped her hands again. “It’s all settled then.”

Keri, Quincy’s sister-in-law, floated into the room with a notebook under her arm. She sidled up to the counter between Claire and Tom. Claire threw an arm around her as if they were old friends.

“What’s this about?” Quincy asked, pointing at the cozy trio.

Keri’s tone was casual and dismissive. “We all got here yesterday. We’ve been hanging out ever since.”

Great. That was just great.

Keri opened the notebook on the counter between them and slid it toward Quincy and Missy. “Here’s the itinerary. Tomorrow morning, we go two ways. Missy is going with Claire and Elaina.” She pointed to Missy’s sister-in-law who waved from her perch at the far end of the counter. Missy flipped her the bird. “And you,” Keri stuck her finger at Quincy, “are coming with me and Jordy.”

“Where are you taking us?” Missy asked.

“Shopping.”

“For what?”

“Dresses, suits, outfits. Whatever.” She waved her hand in the air. “What you want to wear for the wedding. We’re open. But it will be formal wear. No jeans or sundresses.” She stared pointedly at Quincy.

This was getting worse by the minute.

“What’s this?” Missy pointed at the notebook. “Venue walk through? It’s at the same time.”

“Oh, don’t worry about that,” Claire said. “The boys are doing that.”

That obnoxious trill sound interrupted again from

Quincy's pocket. She managed to get the sound turned off and the call rejected in record time, but as she turned to Missy, she couldn't mistake the annoyed purse of her lips.

Missy didn't comment on the call from Gina. Instead, she turned toward her mother and Keri. "Where, exactly, are we holding this shindig?"

Keri flipped a page and tapped at a brochure that was slid into the notebook. Quincy could hardly believe her eyes. It was the fanciest, swankiest, most expensive resort on the island.

"Oh mom," Missy sighed. "This is too much."

Tom's voice boomed through the kitchen. "Not for my only daughter, it's not."

Quincy bit her lip. She had to proceed with caution here. Her instincts to reject all of this, scoop Missy up in her arms, and run out of their home screaming, had to be quelled.

Was this a complete nightmare? Yes. Did she want to be literally sedated for the next seventy-two hours? Also yes. Would she rather still be in Canaima making love to her wife? Hell yes.

But she also wanted Missy's family to like her. She needed to have a relationship with them. And if she was being honest with herself, she wasn't mad at the opportunity to resurrect a relationship with her own family. Even if it killed her.

And it just might.

As if to emphasize how tenuously everything hung above their heads, Jack, peering at her from over Tom's shoulder, winked. The action was not comforting, not in the least.

Quincy took in a deep breath. "Okay. What else do we need to do?"

Missy spun her head, wide-eyed. She obviously wasn't

having the same epiphany as Quincy was about the need to make peace with their families. But they'd talk it through later. Besides, it's not like they had much choice.

For now, Quincy could only provide comfort. She squeezed Missy's hand and returned her attention to Keri.

"Get lots of rest, relax, and just go where we tell you to, when we tell you to." Keri swung the notebook back around so it was tucked up against her. "Okay?"

Quincy inhaled another long, deep breath, mustering every ounce of patience within her. More than that, really. She was summoning courage. The courage to make strangers like her and to give in to her own family's need to embrace her.

It was going to take everything she had.

****

Gabriela's lips turned down into a gorgeous pout. "I couldn't take him to the shelter."

Quincy looked down to the pathetic pup at her feet. Harold lay, sprawled out on the grass in the dog run, tummy up, head to the side, tongue lolling out of his mouth. Missy apparently couldn't resist him. She dropped down to crouch beside the wiry terrier and give his belly a good rub while cooing gently to him.

"I always knew this was a possibility. That it could happen. But I didn't…I mean, who does this?" Quincy scratched her head.

"Only monsters. Yes, monsters," Missy said to Harold in a baby voice. The dog licked her arm and gave her an upside-down smile.

"They came here in person. They asked if he was 'fixed'." Gabriela used air quotes with her fingers. "I told them we'd done a lot of work on his fear of loud noises, but that there was more they would have to do once they got home. I gave them all the information you left and told them they could have up to six free sessions via video chat with you. Just like you said."

"And, I take it, they didn't like that?"

"No. They said they live in the city, and if you couldn't fix him, he was better off here. And they made a show of saying goodbye to the poor thing and then fucking abandoned him."

Missy's baby voice cooed. "Monsters, monsters, big fat monsters. You don't need them, do you, baby?" She leaned her face down so Harold could give her a kiss.

"Please don't take him to the shelter," Gabriela begged. "I'll get him a home. Maybe I'll move to a place where I can have a dog and take him myself."

Gabriela lived in a rental house that didn't allow dogs. And she shared it with the rest of Quincy's staff. They couldn't take Harold in.

But she could. She and Missy could.

Just two-years-old. A sweet and loving boy who got along with all the other dogs. Abandoned by his family because he got scared at loud noises. Quincy and Missy had worked hard with Harold on it for two weeks before they left. And Quincy was certain Gabriela had continued while they were gone.

Gabriela twisted her fingers in front of her. "It happened the day after you left. And I didn't want to bother you. So I stayed at your place with him. I hope you're not mad."

Quincy was shocked that Gabriela looked as if she might be afraid of her reaction. Was she so unreadable that Gabriela didn't realize that she had done exactly what Quincy would want her to do?

Lost in revelations, Quincy was slow to answer, but

Missy voiced what she was thinking. "Of course not." Missy sat on the grass beside Harold, who hopped into the opening between her legs. She looked up at Gabriela. "You did exactly the right thing."

"I bought my own groceries and cleaned everything up. And I cleaned up all his fur."

Quincy stepped forward and placed a hand on Gabriela's shoulder. "I gave you a key and asked you to stay here the first night since Harold's parents weren't arriving until after we left, and I didn't want him to be left alone. Of course it was okay for you to stay longer. We are so grateful that you took care of him. And he's not going to the shelter." Quincy glanced at Missy.

She knew that Missy understood how monumental a moment this was. Quincy had confessed to her the reason she hadn't had a dog of her own. She'd told her it was because she was waiting for a partner to parent a dog with. And now she had one.

Greeted with intense silence, Quincy had no choice but to prompt a response. "Missy?" She made eye contact with her bride. It was clear in that gaze the question was about a lot more than Harold.

"We'll keep Harold. He has a forever home with us now."

****

Quincy reminded Keri and Jordy for the third time, "I really hate this."

"Aunt Q, how do you usually get your clothes?" Jordy asked.

"I just wear what the wardrobe person buys for the show. It's in my contract that I get to keep all the clothes used during shoots."

"Seriously?" The teenager's mouth dropped open dramatically.

Quincy couldn't figure out what could possibly be wrong with that. "Yeah. It makes life easy."

But Jordy's curiosity wasn't satisfied. "What about before the show? What did you do then?"

Keri, who was in the process of swiping through a rack thick with hangers of shirts, piped up to answer her daughter. "Her girlfriends always picked out her clothes. And before that, Olivia and grandma."

"Gina did not pick out my clothes."

Keri ignored her defense. "Speaking of Gina, she quit mentioning you on social media after the wedding announcement, you know?"

"I don't care."

"Bullshit! It's the reason you got married."

"One of them."

Jordy's eyebrows scrunched up. "You like Missy though, right, Aunt Q?"

"I do," Quincy said.

Keri threw a shirt onto the pile slung over her arm. "It's so obvious."

"Is it?"

Keri abandoned the rack she'd been looking through and headed toward the other side of the store where the women's dressing room sat. She just assumed Jordy and Quincy were following in her wake, which of course they were. "First of all, I can see with my own eyes how beautiful your wife is. Second, you look at her like she's a really fine steak."

"I'm a pescatarian."

"Okay, fine, a really delicious fish and chips. Not the point. You basically drool when she's around."

Quincy loped along beside Keri. That was true, but

was it written on her face? Doubtful. "Really?"

"Oh my god, yes." Keri stopped at the dressing room. "I bet you're missing her right now."

She absolutely was.

"What's the plan here?" Quincy reverted the subject back to the clothes. Piles of them lay across both her sister-in-law and her niece's arms.

"Start with this." Keri pulled a pair of pants, a shirt, and a blazer out of her pile and shoved them toward Quincy. "Then come out here and show us what it looks like."

Quincy grabbed the clothes and marched into the dressing room. She hated shopping with a deeply embedded passion. The only time she'd ever even glimpsed joy in the act was when she followed Missy through the gift shop at the resort, watching her sort through straw hats, try on scarves, and make funny faces through a glass bottle filled with what was purported to be "Angel Falls Water."

Even now, a smile threatened as she remembered the bright orange over-sized hoodie Missy finally purchased. She shook her head, trying to focus on the task at hand. As she plunged into the dressing room, a long hallway greeted her, wood slatted doors on either side. At the end stood a second entrance. She jogged to it to investigate. Creaking the door open, she peered into a crook that led right back into the store. She gazed out at the tall shelves of shoes obscuring the view toward the more open clothing racks where Keri and Jordy waited for her.

Abandoning the secret exit for now, Quincy ducked into one of the dressing rooms. When she'd wrestled her way into the first outfit, she glanced at herself in the full-length mirror. It wasn't terrible, actually. The pants were a tad too short for her taste, but that tended to happen. She hadn't bothered to tell Keri that trying to find pants that fit her was one item on a very long list of reasons she disliked shopping.

She gave her image a quick shrug and walked back out to Keri and Jordy. "What do you think?"

Keri's eyebrows puckered up. Jordy's mouth squished to one side. "You hate it?" She guessed.

"Actually, I love it," Jordy said. "Except for the jacket. It's kind of boxy."

Whatever that meant, Quincy didn't really care. It was comfortable, and she thought Missy would like it. That was all that mattered to her.

"I like the jacket," Keri said. "But I hate the pants."

"Too short," Quincy said.

"Oh no. The length is fine, Q. That's the trend these days. No, they just," she tipped her head, "they make your legs look really long."

Quincy was the youngest of her siblings, and Brian was nearly ten years older than her. He'd been with Keri since Quincy was ten, and she was as used to Keri bossing her around as Keri was to Quincy talking back.

"Yeah. Well, they are."

Keri quit scrutinizing her pants and pulled another three articles of clothing from her pile. "Try this one."

Quincy held the hangers in one hand and turned the clothes around so they swished and ebbed. "How do you know whatever we get today will match whatever Missy's getting?"

"Since when do you care about matching?" Keri asked.

Quincy used her free hand to clutch her chest. "You offend me, Keri. It's my wedding. Of course I want to match my bride. Or at the very least, not clash with her."

"It's fine, Aunt Q," Jordy said. "We're getting pics from Hannah's as she tries on dresses." She held up her phone but kept the screen facing away from Quincy. "And they're all off-white or cream so far. Not too much lace. We got this."

There were only a few places on the island they could have taken Missy to find a wedding dress. And by mentioning Hannah's, Jordy had just given up the goods to Quincy.

Keri put her hand on Quincy's shoulder, spun her around so she faced the dressing room, and shoved. "Go try it on."

Quincy bounded into the dressing room with a new spring in her step and deceit on her mind. When she reached the stall, she changed into her own clothes, then slipped out the back door, circled around, left the store, caught a cab, and headed straight for the dress shop.

Ten minutes after giving Keri and Jordy the slip, Quincy stood outside the boutique, peering through the large window. Rather than showcasing a mannequin in a dress, the old-school style store window displayed real customers as they showed off wedding, bridesmaid, and prom dresses on a small, mirror-laden stage. A set of six chairs sat with their backs to the window.

Claire and Elaina were perched in the center two chairs, unaware that Quincy stood a few feet behind them, just a simple pane of glass between them and her. They chatted animatedly, Claire's hands flying in the air as she spoke.

Quincy couldn't hear them, but she imagined they were talking over the details of the wedding. She hadn't understood their enthusiasm at first. Yes, a wedding was worthy of celebration, but a marriage of convenience hardly seemed worth the trouble and extreme expense they were going through.

But, Missy was worth it all. She understood that now.

Missy was worth every penny, every moment, every stressor. And maybe, just maybe, her family felt a bit like that about her too.

Quincy shook that thought away and she waited to see if Missy would emerge from the unseen depths of the store. As she did, she replayed the night before in her mind. After everyone had left, they'd slipped out to the training yard and spoken to Gabriela, then Quincy and Missy had returned to the house, Harold in tow.

They got the pup settled in a crate and talked over the options. In the end, they decided to keep him there for now since he was used to sleeping in one. They'd introduce him to sleeping on their bed slowly, so he was comfortable.

Then Missy and Quincy crawled into bed together, made love, cuddled up, and finally talked about the whirlwind wedding plans while still lulled in a mellow post-sex stupor. Quincy distinctly remembered the way Missy's soft fingers ran slowly along her clavicle, the action keeping her calm even as they ramped up the anxiety by discussing the ambush they'd come home to.

They both agreed the second wedding was going to be stressful for them. They agreed they would go along with it, but promised to take care of each other through the process. Then they sealed that sweet promise with another set of orgasms.

A shiver ran through Quincy as she remembered the sensations roiling through her while she lay at the mercy of her stunning wife. She pictured the way Missy's eyes looked as she trailed kisses down her torso, big brown irises peeking up at her.

"Fuck," Quincy whispered to herself. She opened her eyes and considered leaving. This whole stalker thing was probably a step too far. But then, as she peered through the glass of the store's massive window, Missy stepped out from behind a door and took center stage.

For a long moment she had her back to the window as she stared into a tall mirror. The mirror's frame was visible, but it was angled away, hiding Missy's reflection from view. Dying to know what Missy saw in that reflective glass, Quincy might not survive the suspense.

But then Missy spun around.

She faced her mother and sister-in-law, and unbeknownst to her, Quincy. Missy wore an off-white gown. The shoulders were dropped down, the neckline plunged toward the gentle swell of her pert breasts. Lace covered her waist, a place Quincy had come to appreciate as the sensual connection between two erogenous zones. It then spilled onto the skirt, reaching to the floor.

Missy smiled and twirled, sending the skirt spinning out. Quincy sucked in a breath. Never had she seen anything so beautiful in her life. She might pass out right here, her head bouncing against the concrete and creating a concussion. And that would suck, because then she couldn't marry this beautiful woman all over again.

Chapter 15

Definitely Don't Form an Unhealthy Obsession with Your Fake Wife

This dress was okay, but the first one she'd tried on was 'the one.' Missy would humor her mother and Elaina. This one was clearly their favorite. But then every dress she'd tried on had been their favorite. If she put on a hundred dresses, they would like the hundredth one the best.

In the end, she'd choose that first one, the simple spaghetti strap A-line that reminded her most of the sundress Quincy loved so much. It went nearly to the floor, and still looked like a wedding dress, but it was also very much her style.

"Missy, sweetheart, which one do you think Quincy will like best?"

A part of her hated that her mom was once again putting everyone else's opinion above Missy's. But some of that ancient angst had subsided in the wake of finding a new side to herself in Canaima. And a stronger emotion now took it place. She loved that her mother was including Quincy in the pile of people who got to meddle in Missy's life. "The first one."

"Missy." Elaina's voice was severe. "Can we talk about this marriage a bit?"

The word "no" was stamped on Missy's tongue. She absolutely did not want to talk about her marriage right here in front of her mom while wearing a wedding dress about thirty hours from her second wedding. Just no.

But Elaina didn't wait for consent. She plunged forward. "This is supposed to be a marriage of convenience."

Missy nodded, unable to deny that's what she'd told her family. "Yes, and I went into it with open eyes, Elaina. I knew what I was doing."

"Aha, you knew what you were doing. Past tense."

"What's your point?"

"My point is, you've changed. You're in love with Quincy. Admit it."

Missy froze. The lace of the dress tickled the tops of her feet. The carefully placed lighting above had her breaking out into a sweat. The slick stage floor beneath her allowed the heels she wore to slip just a tiny bit. How did Elaina know?

Her heart thumped in her chest. She was a terrible liar. It would do no good to even attempt it. And yet it felt strange to admit her feelings to her mom and Elaina before she'd spoken them to Quincy.

"Missy?" her mom asked. "Are you?"

Missy swallowed hard. It did nothing to stave off the dryness in her mouth.

Her mother stood and stepped onto the low stage. She took Missy by the shoulders, forcing her to look into her eyes. "Are you in love with Quincy?"

Missy just nodded, unable to put voice to it.

Her mother gathered her into a hug, sending Yasmin, the salesperson, into a fit over the wrinkles she was putting in the dress, and Missy nearly into a coma over the shock. Her mother showed affection in a lot of ways—money, protection, over-the-top worry—but none of them usually involved hugs.

Before she could fully recover, her mother whispered into her ear, "Don't get your heart broken, my sweet girl."

Fifteen minutes later they walked out the bridal shop door, Claire Green still composing herself, and Missy Adams still trying her wrap her head around everything that was happening.

The dress had been purchased and would be picked up the next morning by Elaina. That task over with, as well as the confession she'd been forced to make, Missy felt lighter. She looked forward to spending the rest of the day with Quincy and Harold.

Almost as if she'd conjured her out of thin air, Quincy appeared on the sidewalk in front of the shop.

"What are you doing here?"

Quincy leaned down and kissed Missy on the cheek as she took both her hands. But she didn't speak. Missy understood the signs now. Quincy needed a minute to decide exactly how she wanted to respond. Careful and thoughtful with every word, especially in front of other people, Quincy just required time. So Missy waited.

A car door slammed behind Quincy. Keri and Jordy rushed out, making their way over to the four women gathered in front of the shop.

"Holy shit, Quincy," Keri said.

Jordy laughed breathlessly. "Oh my god, Aunt Q, you are something else."

"What's going on?" Missy's mom asked.

"Seriously, what is happening?" Elaina added.

Jordy pointed at Quincy. "She ditched us at the store soon after she weaseled your location out of us."

"Out of you," Keri said, pointing her finger at her daughter.

"Yeah, me. And she literally ditched us! I mean, I'm kind of impressed."

"I'm not," Keri said.

"Why would you do that?" Elaina asked.

Missy stared up into Quincy's eyes, taking it all in, but still waiting for the response that was just for her.

"Did you see the dress?" Claire asked, her voice cracking as if this were the most important thing in this moment of chaos.

Missy couldn't care less.

"Oh my god!" Keri said. "Quincy, did you?" She turned to the other women. "It took us a while of searching the store before we realized she'd probably come here. She may have been here for a while." She rounded on Quincy again. "Quincy?"

Quincy kept her gaze focused completely on Missy. "Not unless you chose the last one. Maybe I did. Did you pick the last one?"

Missy shook her head. "No, sweetheart. I didn't pick the last one."

"Oh, thank god!" Claire said.

Missy couldn't help the giggle that escaped her. The drama was getting to be a little over the top. "Mom, we're already married. I don't think seeing the dress is the end of the world."

"Ugh. Missy. Please. Let me have this."

Missy laughed again.

Quincy, however, remained still, her expression stoic. Missy reached up and placed one hand on her cheek. "Honey, what is it?"

"The reason I came here."

"Yeah, what was it?"

"I missed you. I wanted to see you."

If she weren't made of solid material. If it weren't a perfect seventy-seven degrees. If she weren't standing on a public sidewalk, Missy would melt at Quincy's feet.

Instead, not caring about witnesses, she threw herself into Quincy's arms and dropped one long, deep kiss on her sweet, handsome wife.

****

The midday sun cooked Uncle Jack and Uncle Henry's patio in a way very similar to how Henry cooked burgers—very thoroughly. Missy longed for a comfy sundress, but she'd been whisked away to the barbeque directly after their adventure at the bridal boutique.

She glared over at Elaina, whom she'd practically begged to let her go home between events so she could exchange her shirt and long pants for a dress, that excuse being only partly true. She also wanted some time alone with Quincy before they were once again surrounded by family.

But it wasn't to be. And now she knew what Quincy's brothers, Brian and Karl, Missy's father, and her intrepid uncles had been up to while they were out shopping.

Streamers dropped down from the patio overhang, and sprays of foil-like things were stuck to the tables which overflowed the deck space and spilled out onto the lawn. Plastic leis, with flowers featuring colors impossible to reproduce in nature, hung over everyone's necks. If this was any indication, the reception was going to be very interesting.

"Your wife watches you." Elaina pointed to where Quincy stood on the other side of the patio.

Even as Quincy spoke to her brother Karl, her eyes wandered to Missy. Their gazes clashed. Quincy winked, creating a fresh flush of heat in Missy's cheeks.

"She does."

"So, you're doing well physically?"

Missy hit her sister-in-law in the arm. "Come on. Don't be weird."

"I'm not being weird. I'm being concerned. You love her, she's attracted to you. These are not the same."

Elaina was right. Attraction, lust, desire, it was all there in spades. But did anything substantial lay beneath that shiny pile of sensation-based emotions?

Missy looked around. This was not the time or the place. "Subject change. Can we talk about this wedding? Everyone is being kinda secretive. What do you know?"

Elaina was in the process of shaking her head when Claire threw open the patio door and announced loudly, "She's here!"

Commotion ensued as a stunning woman stepped through the door. Long, straight, blonde hair streamed behind her tall, curvy figure as she ran full tilt toward Quincy. That swooshy, shiny hair that reached nearly to her waist floated around their bodies as they pressed together, meeting in all the right places.

Olivia. A fire burned in Missy's gut. Insecurity boosted up jealousy and brought it right to the base of her throat. The sensation stung at her eyes, as if she were choking.

"Who the hell is that?" Elaina asked.

"Quincy's best friend."

"Oh man. Has Quincy hit that?"

She had, actually. Thanks for the reminder, Elaina. "They're just friends."

Elaina whistled. "Don't play with me, Missy. I'm bi, and I know exactly how hot that woman is."

Quincy swung Olivia around in a circle. When she put her down, Missy got a clear view of Quincy's face. It was lit up like a diva in a spotlight on stage. Quincy's eyes were wide and sparkling, her cheeks flushed. Missy had never seen Quincy like this before.

Despite the debilitating jealousy, the magnet that was Quincy drew her in. She moved toward her wife, desperate to be closer to her joyous beauty. Quincy didn't see her approach, gaze pinned to Olivia as the blonde told the story of her journey from the mainland.

Missy planted herself beside Quincy, and with the lightest touch, caressed her arm. Quincy immediately turned to her. She looped her arm around Missy's lower back and pulled her into her side.

"Olivia, this is Missy. My wife."

Olivia threw herself at Missy, a whirlwind of blonde hair, curves, and a floral perfume enveloping Missy in a hug so enthusiastic it neared violence. "Holy shit!" She pulled back, grasping Missy by the shoulders. "I can't believe you exist! I was starting to think you were too good to be true!"

Missy swallowed down the insecurity and jealousy that had lodged themselves in her throat. They slid away entirely as Quincy ran gentle fingers along her side. "I'm so happy you two are finally meeting."

"I'm glad I could make it." Olivia took Quincy's chin between her finger and thumb. "It's one thing to have a fake wedding without me, but not this."

What did that mean?

Quincy laughed and batted Olivia's hand away. But her grip on Missy's waist with her other hand didn't loosen. Her thumb found its way under Missy's shirt and the sensation of skin on skin only increased Missy's attention to the spark igniting within her from Quincy's touch.

"Come on, we should introduce you to Missy's family."

Olivia rubbed her hands together as if she were about

to count her winnings at the casino. "Please do!"

****

The revelers lingered long after the last of the burgers had been consumed. And so did Missy's need to be alone with Quincy. Between Quincy's display at the dress shop and her constant touch on Missy's skin as they moved through the party, Missy was a melted candle in need of an even hotter flame.

Fortunately, Olivia ran interference significantly increasing Missy's appreciation of her presence. She grabbed Missy and Quincy by the elbows, explaining to the *Dogs in Paradise* crew members they were talking to that she needed to borrow them for a moment. She ushered them to the side gate and shooed them out before they knew what was happening.

Olivia threw them a wave and a mischievous smile before ducking back into the yard. Missy turned, intending to touch Quincy more thoroughly while they were alone by the side of the house. But Quincy's form disappeared around the garage. By the time Missy had followed her around the corner, Quincy was pulling out two bikes.

She gestured toward Jack's purple and red one. "Shall we?"

Missy jumped on the bike before Quincy could even get seated on Henry's ten speed. "Race you!" She called out as she pulled onto the quiet side street.

Quincy overtook Missy as they approached the turn off to Quincy's property, but she slowed her pace so that they parked the bikes in front of the cottage at the same time. With a wide smile, she held the door for Missy, who plunged into the quiet house.

Quincy threw her arms wide as she waltzed into the living room behind her. "Empty!"

In defiance of this exclamation, Harold ran around the corner and jumped up on them both. While Quincy gave him copious pats, Missy stepped into the kitchen to see if Gabriela was still at the house. A neatly written note on the counter explained that she'd left about an hour before and that Harold had a long walk and dinner.

She spun around to find Quincy and Harold loping into the kitchen. "Gabriela gone?"

"Yes." Missy handed Quincy the note and ducked into Harold's cabinet. She pulled out a hard cheese stick—Harold's favorite—and held it out.

Harold let out a soft cry of delight before snatching the stick from her hand and marching off toward the living room to enjoy his treat.

Quincy dropped the note on the counter and moved with purpose toward Missy. Before she could wrap her arms around her, Missy leaped. Quincy easily caught her, holding all her weight as she planted a sensual kiss in the crook of her neck.

"Oh man, did I need this," Quincy groaned.

Missy stretched her neck to give Quincy better access. "You think we'll make it to the bed?"

Quincy took a step forward, then slid Missy onto the kitchen counter. "Nope. Not gonna make it." She pressed in between Missy's legs, forcing them to widen around her hips and gave Missy an urgent kiss.

Missy ran one hand over the front of Quincy's shirt, following the swell of her breasts. She tugged, pulling the tails out and slid her hand onto Quincy's stomach, but buttons created a frustrating barrier. She leaned back, pulling her lips away from Quincy, who groaned in protest.

"Too many buttons, baby." Her fingers fumbled at the bottom of the shirt.

"I got you." Quincy helped by starting at the top.

Seconds later their hands met. Quincy brushed her fingers along Missy's wrist as she popped the last button and shoved the sides of the shirt away from Quincy's skin.

Missy savored the feel of Quincy, her fingers carefully exploring each dip and rise, as Quincy began her own struggle with fabric. Gentle fingers turned more methodical as she worked to get Missy's pants through the gauntlet of ass and counter.

"I much prefer the dresses." Even as she complained, she hit the mark and slid the pants down Missy's legs, dropping them onto the floor.

Quincy dove back into kissing Missy as her fingers gently stroked Missy's silk panties. Each touch, every taste, and vibrations from the soft moans in Quincy's throat, all of them fueled an explosion growing within Missy. But there was much more than an orgasm barreling her way. The monumental moment now set in motion could not be stopped.

Missy threw her head back and let out a ragged cry. Quincy made a noise of triumph before bending over. Quincy quickly removed the silk panties and was now eye-to-eye with Missy's center, her legs spread open by Quincy's hands on her thighs.

Despite the need rising again inside her as Quincy stared at her with naked longing, Missy needed something richer. Sharp and aching, she tried to voice it. "Quincy," Missy whispered, her voice too weak to come out any louder. "I want to touch you."

"Later, baby. I'm busy." As soon as the words left her mouth, Quincy's lips followed a sinful trail up Missy's right thigh.

Missy braced her hands on the counter behind her in an effort to keep from falling. She threw her head back and let out a low moan as Quincy's ministrations focused on her clit. With no escape from the sensation Quincy sent soaring through her, Missy gave herself over. Quincy pushed her up a mountain of pleasure until the inevitable summit drew near, and she was helpless to stop it.

Could Quincy possibly know how much of Missy she possessed? More than anyone ever had.

As if responding to Missy's thoughts, Quincy moaned and pushed two fingers inside Missy. The sound stroked Missy's core just as Quincy did, and the fuse was lit. Her body and her heart, in sync with one another, blew wide open. Both filled now with just one thing—Quincy.

Quincy straightened, gathering the still shivering Missy to her. Missy pressed her face into the cradle at the joining of Quincy's neck and shoulder. And there she let the shrapnel fly.

"I love you, Quincy. I love you."

Who knew what Quincy might say in response. Maybe something to lighten the moment, or perhaps she'd stay stiff with uncomfortable silence. What Missy had just blurted out was monumental in a way that could not be ignored.

But Quincy's sudden yell was definitely not on the Bingo card.

"Holy hell!" She toppled to the side, leaving Missy alone and exposed on the counter. Missy sat up quickly as something struck her foot. Harold's tail swished erratically while he jumped up on Quincy's bare torso, his excitement at this new game palpable.

Quincy managed to rearrange herself so she sat on the floor. She scooped Harold into her lap and stroked his head. “Calm down buddy. Nothing exciting is happening.”

Missy could not agree with that! She’d been pretty damn excited. She pulled herself off the counter and retrieved her underwear and pants. Quincy didn’t look up as she shoved both on.

Standing there in the kitchen, she stared down at her wife and her dog, both lost in each other. Suddenly cold, and very alone, she moved away, heading outside for a walk around the property.

Quincy was not ready to hear what Missy had said. She’d made a terrible mistake, one she wouldn’t easily be able to rectify.

Chapter 16

Whatever You Do, Don't Fall in Love with Your Fake Wife

Missy had stalked out of the house over an hour ago. She might not have if Quincy had been able to respond to those words. But in the moment, she was too surprised to form a thought. She'd been completely caught up in Missy. The taste of Missy on her tongue, the feel of her quivering around her, and the sound of her voice, wrecked with lust, telling her she loved her. She couldn't have managed words if her life depended on it. And as it turned out, she hadn't needed to. Harold's interruption was welcome.

But now, alone with Harold, Quincy waited to give Missy the speech she'd practiced while Missy was gone. Should she write it down? Naw. That was too impersonal. Instead, she memorized it. First, she'd tell Missy that she was beautiful and kind and made Quincy happy every day they were together. The ending was the most important part. She'd tell Missy what she felt. She'd tell her that she wanted to be with Missy just like Missy wanted to be with her.

Her heart hammered in her chest as the back door opened. She left Harold alone on the couch and moved toward the mud room. Missy sat on the bench, pulling off a pair of sneakers.

"Hey."

Missy didn't look up at her. "Hey. How's Harold?"

"Harold's fine. How are you?"

Missy tucked her shoes under the bench and reached for a pair of rubber sandals she liked to wear around the house. "I'm fine. I filled in some of the holes in the play yard. Those two spaniels we had the week before we left really did a number on it."

Quincy took a deep breath as Missy stood, ready to drop the first line of her speech, but was cut off by Harold's bark. Missy moved past her into the living room. "Is someone at the door?"

As soon as she said it, the bell rang, causing Harold to amp up his barking. Quincy followed Missy as she made her way to the front. She was standing just a few feet behind her, hanging onto Harold's collar as Missy opened the door revealing all the women in both of their families, huddled on the porch in a pack, with Olivia standing at the back and waving her hand in the air as if she were sending a warning that was far too late.

Claire marched into the house forcing Missy, Quincy, and Harold to back out of the doorway in an awkward shuffle. "It's the night before the wedding!"

"We know mom. We're fully aware," Missy said. "And you all have hotel rooms to go to, so what are you doing here?"

Elaina stepped around Claire and placed a hand on Missy's upper arm. "Kidnapping you."

"What?" Missy wrenched her arm back.

"You can't stay here tonight," Keri said. "It's your wedding night."

Missy dropped her head to one side and sighed. "Don't be ridiculous. We're not following some stupid tradition like that."

"Oh yes, we are," Claire said.

"We're having a slumber party at the hotel." Jordy was clearly delighted with this plan. "We got adjoining rooms for all the girls. It's gonna be lit."

"Come on," Claire placed a hand on Missy's back and turned her toward the hallway. "Let's pack you up some things."

Missy shot Quincy one quick look. It was just long enough to register her regret. They weren't going to get to finish that conversation now. Quincy followed Claire and Missy. At the entrance to the spare room, Missy paused. But nothing was in there anymore. The bed was covered in new collars and leashes for Harold, a jacket, and a handful of brand-new toys.

Missy continued onto their bedroom, Quincy and Claire both silently following her. She moved methodically to retrieve her overnight bag and pack it with a handful of items. Quincy bounced on her toes. Missy shouldn't leave like this, with important things unsaid.

"Claire," Quincy said. "Can we get a minute?"

With wide eyes, Claire swiveled her head between Missy and Quincy. She nodded, and stepped out of the room, closing the door behind her. Quincy took a deep breath. Missy finished her packing, zipped her bag, and turned to face Quincy.

"Hey," Quincy said.

"Hey."

"I can't believe they're making you leave."

Missy shook her head. "They're too much."

"We need to talk. About what happened."

"Yeah. We do."

Quincy took a step toward Missy. She could almost reach her, but she kept her hands to herself, for now. "First, I need you to know that you are beautiful and kind and so incredibly thoughtful."

Missy's mouth dropped into a distinct frown. Quincy was saying nice things about her, and she was frowning? What was going wrong here? And if she couldn't get the compliment part right, how was she supposed to convince Missy that she shared her feelings?

She needed a better reaction than this frown. "I'm trying to tell you things here."

"But you're not saying anything."

Quincy stared, mouth dropped open. They were words she spent a lot of time thinking about. Why weren't they good enough?

"You know what," Missy said, "why don't we both just do some more thinking and—"

From her pocket, the familiar trill ring sounded.

Missy moved toward her as she pulled the phone out. "Who is that? They keep calling, and you never tell me who it is. The ring is different—"

Before Quincy could do anything about it, Missy was leaned over, staring right at her screen. An image of Gina, hair flying around her shoulders, lips turned up in a sly smile, stared back behind the notification of the incoming call. Quincy hit the reject button quickly and shoved the phone back in her pocket.

"All those calls have been Gina?"

"Yeah."

"What does she want?"

"I have no idea. I haven't answered any of the calls."

Missy stuck a hand on her hip. "You aren't the least bit curious?"

"No."

"But you didn't block the number."

That was a valid point. One Quincy had no defense for. She could have blocked Gina's number a long time ago.

But definitely when she started calling during the honeymoon. Why the hell hadn't she done that? It certainly would have made this moment less awkward.

"Have you been in communication with her lately?"

"No. I just told you that I never answer the calls. This conversation is getting off the rails. Can we start over?"

A bang on the door prevented Quincy from getting to hear Missy's response. Missy grabbed the overnight bag off the bed and stalked to the door. She threw it open. "I'm ready to go, Mom."

Ten minutes later, Quincy was sitting at the kitchen island across from Olivia nursing a Gin and Tonic.

"So, are we going to talk about that phone call?" Olivia asked.

"There's nothing to talk about since I didn't answer it."

"Except that I heard that phone ring with Gina's ringtone while you were in the bedroom with Missy. Then, she comes running out of the room. So, even if you didn't pick up the phone, shit obviously went down over the call."

"Missy accused me of being in contact with Gina."

Olivia shrugged. "There's obviously a lot of feelings between you two, that I'm guessing you haven't discussed at all."

"How do you know that?"

"I know you, and I know what I saw. I'm guessing that instead of talking about everything, you two are just banging it out." She slapped her hand on the counter. "Which is very fun, I'll grant you, but doesn't resolve anything. So now everybody has messed up feelings they haven't told the other person about, and bam." She hit the counter again. "Enter the ex. It's like a romance novel."

Olivia wasn't wrong. If Quincy were reading this, she'd be yelling at the main characters to just have a fucking conversation already. "You think I should call Missy?"

"Not unless you know exactly what to say."

Quincy never knew what to say, her secret sauce was in actions, not words. Missy loved it when Quincy showed up at the dress shop or when she'd helped her get into that boat to Angel Falls.

"I need to figure that out."

"So call Gina."

"What? You want me to call Gina? How does that help?"

"You need to close that chapter of your life so you can start a new one with Missy. Missy obviously feels that way, or she wouldn't have been alarmed by the call from Gina."

"Why would Missy think that Gina was even a factor? I never talk about her."

Olivia gently slapped the top of Quincy's head. "Duh? You got fake married to Missy because of Gina."

"Only partly."

"I'm going to punch you."

Aside from the phone calls that interrupted her honeymoon bliss, Quincy hadn't thought about Gina. But Olivia was right. Gina was a problem that Quincy had the power to solve. Actions over words, right?

"Okay." She fished out her phone, called, and hit the speaker. She dropped the phone on the counter between them as if it might burn her.

"Q!"

Her own voice was flat and stale compared to Gina's excited tone. "Hi, Gina."

"Oh my god, I just heard you're getting married tomorrow."

"I already got married. Didn't you hear that?"

Across the counter, Olivia rolled her eyes, expressing what Quincy was feeling. Of course Gina knew they were already married. Everyone did. She was playing dumb for a reason.

"Oh right. And this is like a…what? Vow renewal? Seems kind of soon for that." Gina laughed that high pitched nervous giggle that always wore on Quincy's nerves.

"No. This time we're just doing it in the presence of family. This one is for them."

"Why do it at all?"

In twin movements, both Quincy and Olivia jerked their heads back.

"Excuse me?" Quincy asked.

"Why are you marrying this person, Q?"

Quincy looked to Olivia for help. "Tell her the truth," Olivia said.

"Is that Olivia?"

"Yes, I'm here. Hey Gina."

"Hey! You came out for the fake wedding, too?"

Quincy's blood boiled. It was sudden and unexpected. Was it Gina that brought this out in her or the question? She wasn't entirely sure. Either way. She'd end this.

"It's not fake."

"Q. Please. I'm not stupid. I know you. And I don't believe for one minute that you fell in love with some young kid in a matter of weeks and wanted to get married. That's not you."

"You're right. It's not. And when I first proposed to Missy—who's not a kid, by the way—I was doing it partially in reaction to you going out into the press telling people we were getting back together." She had to admit that to Gina to get the weight off her shoulders. Now it was dissipating into the universe. It wouldn't be a factor anymore. Check that one off.

"I knew it." Air hit the phone hard as Gina huffed. "Q, baby. You don't have to do this to get me back."

Of course her needed confession was taken by Gina as a desire to re-ignite their flame. Not surprising, Gina had always been a self-centered person. She'd always framed Quincy's actions in terms of herself.

Maybe she was just as bad. When they were together, Quincy hadn't spent time thinking about how her actions would affect Gina. When Gina read into them, she'd always been frustrated and annoyed. Many times over, she'd told Gina that she did things for her own reasons, not other people's.

But now she thought about Missy when she did things. It was just one more bit of evidence that she'd never felt about Gina the way she felt about Missy. She caught Olivia's righteous smirk and knew that's exactly what she'd wanted her to realize in this little exercise with Gina.

"I didn't marry her to get you back. I actually did it to get you off my back. I don't want to get back together with you. I wanted to put an end to the speculation on social media so I could move on with my life."

"And you don't think that's kind of drastic? You claim you don't want me back so much that you got married to a stranger. Not buying it."

Where was her anger? Gina, like this, usually created a fire of rage in her gut. But there was nothing there. "That's not accurate. But if it were, it doesn't matter now."

"It does matter, baby. You don't have to be stuck in this marriage. You can get out of it and come back to me."

"No, Gina. Listen to me. It doesn't matter now because

I want to be with Missy, in a way I never wanted to be with you. A forever way. So, thanks for calling, but I need to go make love to my wife." She hit the end button just as Olivia erupted into applause.

****

"What kind of fresh hell is this?" Olivia moaned. Her hand flopped off the couch, hitting Quincy in the face.

The doorbell rang again, pounding through Quincy's brain like a kid with his first drum set. Harold's frantic barking accompanied it.

Quincy sat up, her body aching from the hard floor. Had she fallen asleep here in the living room? She reached out blindly. "Harold, baby, come here." His body dropped beside her, and his tongue met her cheek. She patted him.

"It's okay, baby. Relax. Shit. I didn't put you in your crate last night." She'd wanted him to feel safe all the time, at every moment. Sleeping in the crate was part of that safety. She couldn't afford to screw up with him this early in his time with them.

She checked him out, and he seemed okay. Eyes bright, tongue lolling to one side. She glanced at his crate. The door stood wide open, revealing his favorite toy tucked inside. He'd probably slept there anyway.

"Make it stop," Olivia groaned, smacking her on the face again as the doorbell pealed for a third time.

Harold didn't bark this time. Proud of him, Quincy dropped a kiss on his head and looked around at the wreckage. Three empty bottles of wine sat on the coffee table beside her like evidence in a crime. Yep. That's what happened. Not willing to go into her cold bed alone, she'd pissed away the evening with Olivia and way too much pinot.

"Quincy, you in there?"

"Fuck." Quincy forced her aching body into a standing position. "That's Jack."

If he was here banging on her door at ass-o'clock in the morning, was something wrong with Missy? Had Missy changed her mind? Was she a runaway bride? Had she asked Jack to come over here with an annulment agreement? Was she hurt? Had the limo crashed? Had crazy-ass Keri taken her into town on a drunken bachelorette party and lost her somewhere on the island?

She opened the door. Jack stood there, alone, holding a paper tray with three cups of coffee. Harold ran past him and out into the yard to his favorite tree.

"Good morning."

"Seriously?"

Jack grinned. "You look like you had a rough night. I brought an offering." He held up the tray.

"I see that." Quincy glanced past him. Harold met her gaze, trotted back to the door, slipped past Jack, and jumped on the couch to give Olivia a tongue bath. "Come in."

As she shut the door behind him, she couldn't help but ask. "Is Missy okay?"

"She's fine, as far as I know." He handed one of the cups to Olivia, who was struggling to sit up. Jack swung around and handed another cup to Quincy. Then he dropped into the floral print chair, hefting his own coffee and dumping the paper tray on the coffee table beside the empty wine glasses. "Probably in better shape than you."

Quincy shoved Olivia's legs aside and plopped down on the end of the couch closest to Jack. "We might have gotten a little carried away."

"Cold feet?" He took a sip of his coffee casually, as if

he hadn't just laid that bomb on her.

"Why would I have cold feet about marrying a person I'm already married to?"

"I don't know, Quincy. I married for love. I don't have any other understanding of marriage."

She got what he was saying. But things were different now. Her marriage was no longer one of convenience. And even though she and Missy had agreed to keep the changed nature of their relationship to themselves, she wasn't sure that was possible anymore.

She wished she could talk to Missy.

"I don't have cold feet. I didn't want to go to bed alone last night. And this one," she pointed at Olivia, "is a very bad influence."

"It's true. I am." Olivia patted Harold on the head.

Jack took a long sip from his coffee. "I got a late-night phone call last night."

That was weird. "Okay."

"From your ex. Gina."

Quincy's insides roiled. "What?"

"Yeah. She called me. Got my number from a mutual friend in L.A. I've actually met her before. I think I told you that once."

Quincy racked her brain. Did she know that? Yes. Jack mentioned it one night over drinks. Long before Missy touched down on the island and snuck into her life.

"I think you mentioned that you were introduced to Gina at a fundraiser once. So, what did she say to you last night?"

"Said she talked to you."

Olivia said, "Oh yeah. Bitch called."

Quincy went for a more diplomatic response. She didn't know how close Jack was to the friend that was the mutual connection between himself and Gina. That could change a lot, no matter how tight she thought she was with Jack. "I talked to her."

He sipped his coffee again, deep brown eyes, not unlike Missy's, piercing her over the top of the cup.

"What did she tell you?" Quincy asked.

"She told me about your conversation."

"Stop playing with me, Jack. What did she say?"

"I want to hear it from you."

Whatever Gina said, it was a lie. But it was one Jack believed. His opinion mattered in terms of how it might transfer to Missy. She loved her uncle and put him on a pedestal. Once upon a time, Jack coming to Quincy with ridiculous conspiracies from her unhinged ex would have been easy to laugh off. Now it was far more serious.

"I told her I was happily married, and that tomorrow I'm re-marrying my beautiful wife. She wanted to get back together with me, and I told her no way. And that's it."

Jack studied her. "I see."

"You wanna tell us what Gina said to you?" Olivia asked.

Jack sat back in the flowery chair that Missy had claimed as her own since moving in. Instead of her uncle lounging there, Quincy could picture Missy, her feet tucked up under her, lying back with her Kindle on her lap.

Jack let out a long breath before telling his story. "She said you called her. Did you call her?"

"I called her *back*. She's been calling me for weeks."

"Then why did you finally call back last night? Why the night before your wedding?"

Anger rose again like bile in her throat. "First of all, I don't like the accusatory tone. And second, I don't see anything wrong with seeking a little closure before my wedding."

"Normally I might agree. Under normal circumstances. But these aren't normal, are they?"

That was clearly meant to bait her, and she wasn't taking it. She glared at Jack.

Jack held her gaze as he continued. "She says you called her and wanted to know if she still wanted you. She was concerned about Missy after that call. She wanted me to know about her concern."

"That bitch!" Olivia exploded off the couch, upsetting Harold and sending him running into Quincy's lap.

Quincy pulled Harold close and stroked his fur. "Not only is that a lie, it's a stupid one. Sounds like something a middle schooler would come up with. You believed this drivel?"

Jack's gaze swiveled from Olivia to Quincy and back a few times. The stark difference in Olivia's ferocious reaction and Quincy's almost amused calm obviously affected him. "I believe you. But why did she call me and tell me this lie?"

"It's obvious, Jack," Olivia said. "She's fucking with Quincy. The woman she wants back, and can't have back."

"Part of the reason you and Missy got married was because of Gina," Jack said.

Quincy bit her lip. She needed to stop this train, and there was one sure way to do that. But would she be breaking her pact with Missy to not tell their families? Maybe, given the circumstances, Missy would agree that it had to be done. Quincy kissed the top of Harold's head and made up her mind. If Missy got mad, she'd take her punishment and come up with a sweet, sexy way to make it up to her. "It was originally a reason for the marriage. But none of it matters anymore."

Jack sat forward. "And why's that?"
"Because I'm in love with your niece, Jack."

Chapter 17

It's Crucial to Know Exactly What You're Getting into as You Plan to Walk Down the Aisle

Some horrific substance floated over Missy's head like a toxic cloud. "Keri, please. I'm going to suffocate."

"Jesus, mom," Jordy said, flailing her hand around her head. "Can we not kill the ozone layer today please?"

Missy could see Keri's eyes roll in the reflection of the mirror in front of her. "Fine." She set the bottle of hair spray down on the counter. "I was done anyway."

"Thank you." Missy reached up to touch her curls in an attempt to determine just how ceramic they were. "I need to breathe."

Keri shoved her hand down. "Don't touch."

"Is this going to put a damper on sex later?" Missy asked. "Because honestly, that's what I'm looking forward to most today." A memory shot through her from yesterday afternoon. Quincy bent over her, Missy, bare ass on the kitchen counter lost in absolute bliss. And those words, spoken in a moment of utter honesty.

"Missy, please. I am too old for this conversation."

"Mom, you're not," Missy said. "And don't pretend you thought I wasn't having sex with my wife."

"Oh, she probably did." Elaina said from her perch in the corner of the room. "I'm pretty sure she thinks Matt and I sleep in separate beds. She has a weird block about this."

"Well, I have sex with my wife, mom. And I really, really like it." Missy grinned at her reflection in the mirror. Keri smirked back at her.

Keri stepped into the mirror's reflection, expression serious. "So, do you have feelings for Quincy?"

Missy had already spilled the beans to her mom and Elaina yesterday. But she'd planned to keep to her agreement with Quincy and not tell anyone else, at least not until after she'd talked to Quincy about it. But instead of having that conversation, she'd blurted out that she was in love with Quincy. Now she was telling that secret to Quincy's own family.

This was messy. But by the look on Keri's face, it was too late to do anything about it. "I do. And I told Quincy so yesterday."

Keri's eyes grew wide, an indication to Missy that maybe Quincy's emotional unavailability was more stark an obstacle than she thought. Rather than march down that terrifying path, she shifted the conversation. "Jordy, did you find out where the reception is being held yet?"

"I'm not allowed to say where it is. But it's a big, like, outdoor-kinda room," Jordy said.

"That's enough, dear," Missy's mother said. "The bottom line is that it's a gorgeous spot for a sunset reception."

"Thank you, Mom. For all of this. It's going to be great."

"It is," Elaina said. "But, um, speaking of the whole you-have-feelings-for-Quincy thing. There's something I should tell you."

That sounded ominous. Missy instinctively moved her hand to run it through her hair, but Claire slapped it away.

"Well, tell us," Claire said, adjusting a few curls.

"Jack got a call from Quincy's ex-fiancée last night."

That made no sense. "I know Gina called Quincy, but why the hell did she call Uncle Jack?"

"Jack and Gina know each other from back in L.A.," Elaina explained.

Why hadn't Uncle Jack ever mentioned that? It seemed like pretty damn important information.

But the even more essential question remained: why hadn't Quincy told her that the frequent caller with the high-pitched ringtone was Gina? And why hadn't she blocked Gina's number?

She tried to keep her expression neutral. "What did Gina tell Jack?"

"I don't know everything." Elaina's eyes slid to the floor.

"What do you know?"

"Just that Quincy called Gina last night."

Missy could rationalize this in her head. Quincy had never expressed any regret over ending things with Gina. On the face of it, this was not a big deal. But the sweat that was starting to bead underneath the layers of makeup on her forehead didn't care about logic.

Her family didn't need to know that anxiety was roaring through her like an unwelcome, but deeply familiar, old house guest. "So what? She's allowed to call anyone she wants. Especially the night before her wedding. If I had a significant ex, I might do the same thing."

Her mother gazed at her, naked concern painted on her face. "You're not upset?"

"Of course not. This is completely unnecessary drama. What's next? I suppose you all want to throw three more layers of make-up on me." She swung back around to the mirror. "Let's get started. Also, I'm hungry. Is there lunch?"

"I ordered something," Jordy said. "It'll be here soon."

"Jordy, why don't you go check on the food," Keri suggested.

Jordy whined about it for a minute but eventually left. As soon as the door closed, Keri turned on Elaina. "I don't like this shit. Quincy is a good person."

"No one said she isn't." Elaina stood toe to toe with the other woman as if they were about to do battle.

Missy groaned. She did not need a sister-in-law showdown.

Elaina stuck her chin in the air. "But I don't know how Quincy feels about Missy."

"Stop!" Missy shot out of her seat and squeezed between the two women like a referee at a hockey game. "I am a grown-ass woman. And I have been married to my wife for weeks. We've spent every moment together. Twenty-four seven. And I don't need any of you," she waved her arm around the room, "worrying about this. This is my business."

The silence that blanketed the room could have smothered a fire. And maybe it did, because no one spoke.

"Listen. We have a little time, yeah?" Missy asked.

"Sure," Elaina said.

"I'm going to go call Gabriela and check on Harold. She's supposed to be bringing him later, and I need to remind her about some things that should go in the puppy diaper bag."

Every single person in the room rolled their eyes, and Keri mumbled about treating the dog like a human baby. But no one argued with her.

"I'll be back." Missy scooped her phone off the table and marched through the door of the room, not caring that she was only wearing a hotel bathrobe. She passed by a confused-looking Jordy and knocked on room 314.

Her father swung the door open. Before his bewildered expression could give way to a question, she spoke. "Dad. I need your room."

Her father, far smarter than anyone else on the planet, kissed her cheek as she moved past him, grabbed his wallet, and left.

Missy paced around the space for a few minutes. She needed time to breathe. Her parents' room held two queen beds, each with a suitcase spilled out on its surface. She rounded each one, then crossed the room, then circled back again. She made the tour three times before stopping at the foot of one of the beds and pulling out her phone.

While this wedding wasn't the ultimate countdown, since she and Quincy were already legally locked together, it did mean something. Their first wedding had been a transaction, no more impactful than a visit to the ATM. But things were different now. Even if Quincy didn't love Missy, she had slept with her. And their lovemaking wasn't some fast and furious way to get off with the closest available human. It wasn't. It couldn't be. It was more.

But did Quincy feel for her anything close to what she felt for Quincy? Perhaps. It wasn't like there hadn't been signs. On the other hand, she'd kept those calls from Gina a secret, she'd stared at Missy like a deer in headlights when she made her impulsive confession of love, and she'd talked to Gina last night. Gina, the woman who had shared years with Quincy, who no doubt knew her so much better than Missy did.

Missy pulled out her phone and dialed Quincy. The ringing continued for an impossibly long time. The wait was painful. Finally, a voice answered. "Hello?" Only it wasn't the voice she wanted to hear.

"Um. This is Missy."

"Hey, Missy, it's Olivia."

"Can I talk to Quincy?"

"'Fraid not. She's trapped in a dressing room with a psycho armed with pins and a sewing needle at the moment. Plus, I've been given strict instructions not to let you two talk until the vows."

Surely Olivia had Quincy's best interest in mind. Which meant she might be Missy's best bet for getting information. "Um, well, there's something I really wanted to talk about before the wedding."

"Is it about the call from Gina last night?"

If she couldn't talk to Quincy, maybe Olivia could give her a little peace of mind. "Yeah. What do you know about it?"

"Have you talked to your Uncle Jack?"

"Uncle Jack? No. I haven't seen him all day."

"Okay. Don't worry. Just talk to your uncle. He'll tell you everything you need to know. See you later, sweetie." And she hung up.

Missy stared at the phone in her hand. The yearning to talk to Quincy, to hear her voice, to get reassurance from her lips, had not been quelled. And now she had a new assignment. Find Uncle Jack.

Missy swung the hotel room's door open so hard it slammed against the wall. She hoped to find her father on the other side of the door. She could imagine him just standing in the hall, leaning against the pink and green paisley wallpaper, waiting for his daughter to emerge and tell him she needed him to immediately find his brother.

But the hall was empty.

Panic rose through Missy's body like a wave building on its race to the shore. She knew this feeling. And she knew she needed to deal with it right away.

She needed answers.

A lone tear fell from her right eye. She didn't bother to catch it. She let it run over the makeup that had been applied to her face like cement with a trowel. The door to her parents' hotel room clicked shut behind her, snapping her focus back to her task.

Find Uncle Jack.

Her hand was still positioned in a death grip around her phone. She brought it up and dialed Jack's number, even as she moved down the hall toward the stairwell. If Jack answered, she didn't want to lose him in the elevator.

But he didn't answer. Straight to voicemail. As she tromped down the stairs, she dialed Uncle Henry and received the same result. Rounding the last set of stairs, she called her father.

"Hi, sweetie."

"Dad, where did you go?"

"Honey, I thought you wanted time alone."

"I did, but…," Missy stopped when she hit the final landing and took a deep breath. She could work through this. "Where are you right now, Dad?"

"With your mom and your new in-laws. We arranged a meet-up before the wedding, but I was running late because I had a work call. Anyway, we're all at this cute little bar. It's not far away, though. Don't worry. We won't be late to the ceremony. I'll be there to walk you down the aisle."

"Is Uncle Jack with you?"

"No, he and Henry are at the reception spot doing some last-minute things. Why?"

"Where is the reception?"

A strange sound came over the phone, almost as if it had been dropped.

"Oh no you don't!" Her mother's voice echoed over

the phone. "We told you the reception is a surprise. You don't get to go having a sneak peek."

"Mom, I don't want to peek. I just really need to talk to Uncle Jack."

"And there will be plenty of time at the reception. Love you!"

And then her mother hung up.

Missy stared at the phone. All she could do now was to follow the string of clues that had been left like breadcrumbs for her to follow.

****

Missy stood in a glass encased sunroom, sweat dripping between her breasts, beading at her forehead, and making her feet slide around in her sandals.

Elaina put the finishing touches on her make-up while her mother fanned her gently with a resort brochure. "Don't want to mess up the hair," she said when Missy asked if maybe she could pick up the pace so actual airflow occurred around her.

Since her hair was basically glued in place, it seemed completely unreasonable to Missy that she couldn't get some relief from the heat. But then again, everything seemed unreasonable to Missy at that moment.

Soon she would walk down the aisle. She hadn't found her uncle. And she really needed to know what this big secret he had was.

Her anxiety was stuck at moderate, which was not ideal, but better than it could have been. She did some of the breathing exercises Quincy had taught her on the boat to Angel Falls. Didn't help.

"I remember my wedding day," her mother said. "I remember every single detail. The dress. The flowers. The dancing."

"Hmmm." Elaina hummed as she gently brushed at Missy's cheek with what had to be the one hundredth application of blush. "My clearest memories are of the things that went wrong." She pulled her hand away from Missy as she chuckled. "Like the stray dog that wandered into the church just before the ceremony."

They all turned to look at Harold. He was curled up on a bed in the corner of the room, soft snores emitting from him. Twenty minutes ago, Gabriela had delivered Harold, who was freshly bathed and looking smart with a bow tie around his neck. It had been Quincy's idea to include him in the ceremony, which was a definite checkmark on the "things I love about my wife" list for Missy.

Missy took another deep breath and plunged into the conversation. Might as well. Nothing else she could do at this point. "I remember when the stray dog crashed your wedding. She was a mid-sized mixed breed with matted fur. Pretty well nourished though."

"Oh my god. Of course you remember every detail about the dog," Elaina said. "And of course you were the one who walked in and saved the day after the boys spent twenty minutes chasing the poor thing through the pews."

She smiled as she remembered cuddling the pup throughout the wedding ceremony and reception, then taking her to the vet and groomers, going through the process of attempting to find her owners, and eventually rehoming her with the kind couple who had been on the hunt for a dog to dote on after their last one passed. "She was just scared. Tinker is a good, sweet girl. I saw her last time I visited Anne and Kim."

"You're a dog whisperer," Jordy said.

"Not as good as Quincy." Missy couldn't repress the sigh that escaped her lips. There were so many amazing things about her wife. If only she didn't have a giant wall around her heart.

Chapter 18

Relax and Enjoy the Wedding

Olivia was still trying to brush dog hair off Quincy's pants as they walked toward the resort entrance. But Quincy didn't see the point. Harold was in the wedding party. He'd probably barrel down the aisle to her and immediately re-deposit more fur.

She shook her head, but her smile was too big, her heart too happy for anything other than an amused, "You're ridiculous."

"Quincy!"

Quincy stopped short of the door. She had planned to walk in the front, through the resort, and out to the private beach for the ceremony. She had about 15 minutes to get there. But her name being called in a deeply familiar voice changed her course.

She waved to Olivia to go on without her before moving cautiously over to her brothers. They stood in the slatted shade of a palm tree wearing matching white button-up shirts and linen pants.

Brian was just a couple inches taller than Karl, a feature that allowed him to lean one elbow on Karl's shoulder. The dark curls he inherited from their mother matched Quincy's, while Karl's blond locks were straight like their father's.

She moved to stand with them, the three forming a small circle. To an observer they must look like a matching set, so many shared features. The same sharp chin, the same eyes, even a similar way of standing. It was all there to see.

So sharp it nearly toppled her over, an ache hit Quincy in the chest. She loved these two people with every fiber of her being. They were the only other people on the planet who understood what it had been like to be the children of Kyle and Anita Adams.

But loving them in the wake of their parents' death had been too raw, too hard. It had been easier to distance herself from the emotion, to find solace in numbness. Now they stood here in front of her, dopey and stupid, and immaculately imperfect. Karl grinned at her, and she could see the chip in his front tooth from when he fell out of a tree in the front yard, a coconut still clutched in his hands. Brian tossed his head, and the mop of hair hanging over his forehead moved just enough that she could make out the scar that he got when he was attempting to teach her to fly fish, and her hook went awry.

Something snapped inside her. The sound reverberated through her skull and the vibration from the break echoed across her skin. In that one moment, she was freed.

"I love you." The words came out in a whisper so soft she wasn't sure they heard them. Stepping closer, she said it again. "I love your stupid faces."

A tear sprang in Brian's eye, and he lunged forward, scooping her up in a massive bear hug. Her face was buried in his chest, but she still heard Karl's voice break as he said. "Your face is stupider than mine." Then his chest was covering her back, and his arms were somewhere in the mix.

A million things ran through her mind: childhood memories, young adult horrors, and her mistakes, not the least of which was refusing to open her heart to any woman. That pattern ended today.

****

Quincy's knees nearly buckled. Missy, draped in low-slung lace and silk, arm in arm with Tom, moved toward her. Curls dripped from a globe of hair perched on Missy's head. The dark spirals accentuated her long neck and framed either side of her high cheekbones. Her rich brown eyes met Quincy's unflinchingly.

Quincy shivered. Her whole being was possessed by Missy, who moved slow and sensuous like molasses being dropped from a spoon. Every step she took brought her closer to Quincy's arms, which twitched with the need to reach out to her.

It didn't matter that the legalities had been settled for weeks. This ritual was different. This was what Quincy had imagined that glorious day in June 2015. This was what flashed through her head when she heard about the supreme court decision that legalized gay marriage: watching the woman she loved walk toward her as they were about to say vows that would seal them together in an ancient ritual that had, for most of Quincy's life, been unavailable to her.

She probably had the goofiest grin on her face. If physics would allow, she'd also be floating, hovering over the sand, her head about to hit the flowers clinging to the wedding arch above her.

Missy and Tom reached her. As Missy turned to Tom and shared a moment with her father, Quincy drew in a deep breath. It didn't matter that they were already married. This was different. This was real.

Missy turned back, and Quincy reached out her hand. Missy took it, and Quincy couldn't help but squeeze those soft, long fingers as she peeked at Missy's face—so serious, her mouth in a straight line, her eyes wet and wide.

Quincy needed Missy to smile. Her own grin couldn't get any bigger. But Missy was swimming in anxiety right now. It was written all over her, and it was all wrong. She should be happy, living this perfect moment with Quincy.

Quincy turned to the officiant. "Can we have a minute before you start?"

Without question, the woman nodded, staying quiet. Quincy pulled Missy forward, taking both her hands and drawing her close. She leaned in, putting her lips next to Missy's ear.

"I didn't get a chance to tell you this, but I'm so happy I get to do this all over again with you."

She leaned back to look into Missy's eyes. They were softer, calmer. But her mouth was still pinched and unsmiling. So, Quincy leaned back in and whispered in her ear. "Because this time it's different. I feel that. I hope you feel it, too."

When she pulled back, Missy nodded. She bit her lower lip, and a tear hovered above the lashes of her right eye.

"Are you ready to do this?" Quincy asked.

Missy nodded again, and finally, a smile spread across her lips. It was soft and understated, but Quincy would take it. She turned to the officiant. "We're ready."

"Welcome everyone." The woman's voice was smooth, clear, and easily heard over the crashing of waves on the beach. She made a small speech about the meaning of marriage that was surely sweet and impactful, but was lost on Quincy as she was too busy staring at Missy to fully absorb every word.

Missy's dark eyes seemed to be examining her in

return. They moved around her face, the edges slightly squinted. With the sun well on its way to setting, the orange glow couldn't be the cause. Something was going through Missy's head. If only Quincy could reach in, pull out those thoughts, and examine them herself.

They had worked through everything that had plagued them during the honeymoon and had settled into a comfortable place with one another. What happened last night had been a bump in the road. But Olivia said that was settled too. Some new, and as yet unknown, issue must be reeling through the cogs of Missy's mind now.

Quincy was called back to the ceremony by the officiant saying her name. She jerked her head to the right, ripping her gaze away from Missy. She needed to repeat the vows. That she would gladly do. And this time they would mean so much more.

She gazed into Missy's eyes, squeezed her hands, and told her she would love, honor, and cherish her for as long as she could. Those were the words. Not for as long as we both shall live, but as long as we could. Quincy vaguely remembered Missy's parents talking about the choice of vows. But they didn't bother to ask Quincy and Missy which they would prefer.

At time Quincy was too focused on Missy's happiness to care, and Missy said that she was happy to let their families pull the strings on this second wedding. But now the words felt wrong. Sure, they would have been perfect the first time they said these vows, but not anymore.

She said them, though. And Missy said them, too. And they stared at each other as they slipped rings—new, shiny rings Claire had chosen—onto each other's fingers. Then the officiant pronounced them spouses and said they could kiss.

Quincy leaned forward gratefully, touching Missy's

lips with her own. At first Missy just gave her a peck and moved away. But Quincy wrapped her arm around Missy's lower back and pulled her forward. She looked into her eyes, silently begging for more.

Missy smiled and tipped her head, giving Quincy what she really wanted. Quincy sighed into the kiss.

Perfect.

****

Torches and bonfires lit the open-sided tent on the beach that hosted the reception, creating an intensely romantic atmosphere. The canvas and flower-draped area erupted into applause as they entered. Missy's hand squeezed hers, and Quincy squeezed back as they moved through a split in the crowd.

Well, "crowd" was a generous word. Their friends, family, and the show's employees gathered on the island made up thirty people, tops. But in the tent packed with round tables, it seemed like a lot more. And they were loud. Her brothers shouted and whistled, and Quincy couldn't help but grin. Her stupid, obnoxious brothers were here, celebrating this important day with her, and it was so right.

They were seated and promptly served a meal that fit her diet but not Missy's. The error, it turned out, had to do with Claire's belief that Missy had never really turned. Regardless of what that meant for Missy's compounding trauma, it meant that her wife was left with nothing but green beans and a salad to eat.

Quincy, who was willing to strong arm everyone for Missy's happiness and delay the toasts, managed to text the owner of Stevie's and get a special delivery. Missy nearly broke into tears when the veggie lasagna was presented to her.

She was the most vibrant, beautiful woman Quincy had ever seen.

When her plate was nearly cleaned, Missy pushed it aside and called out to Tom. “Okay, Dad. Go!”

Tom stood up from his seat beside Claire on the other side of Missy and beat his fork against his glass with such fervor Quincy worried he would shatter it. When he had everyone’s attention, he began.

“There are three days in my life I will never forget. The day my daughter was born. The day she came out to me. And this day.”

The beginning promised a tear-jerker of a speech, and Tom didn’t disappoint. By the end of his fifteen-minute diatribe, everyone was in tears, including Quincy, and especially Missy. Missy hugged her father, and they had a moment.

Watching them created an echo of a pain in Quincy’s heart, like the phantom ache of a lost limb. She searched the crowd until she met Brian’s gaze. They exchanged a watery smile. She sniffed and turned her attention back to Tom just in time to see him handing her the microphone.

She stood with the microphone in her hand, completely uncertain what to say. Missy looked up at her expectantly, and her brain completely stalled. Nothing. Absolutely nothing came to mind. After at least ninety seconds of awkward silence, she forced herself to speak.

“Well thanks, everyone, for coming to this…our wedding…I mean our second wedding.”

There was a tinkling of laughter that rippled through the tent followed by a horrendous crash. A server had toppled a tray of dirty plates, sending them clattering to the ground in a cacophony of sound.

Harold, who had been sleeping under the table at

Missy's feet, jolted out from under the tablecloth and bolted into the main part of the tent, taking the cloth with him and raining champagne flutes and unused silverware in his wake.

Fortunately, he was too far ahead of his destruction to have been harmed by any of it. But by the time Quincy rounded the table in pursuit, he had weaved his way through the tables, dodging all his would-be captors as they lunged for him.

The cake table sat beside one entrance to the tent, and Harold made a beeline for it. His little body was moving fast when he slammed into one leg of the round table, sending the cake crashing down. Again, he managed to dodge the falling debris, and slipped out of the tent unscathed.

After making her way through the cake wreckage, Quincy emerged from the tent with Missy on her heels and scanned the beach even as she tried to will her eyes to adjust to the darkness faster.

"There!" Missy pointed to the distinctive terrier silhouette trotting along the water's edge.

Quincy took off in that direction. "He's slowing down."

Missy's voice came from just behind her. "Thank god. Running in this dress is a bitch."

Quincy didn't doubt that, and between her pants and her longer legs, she pulled ahead of Missy as she all out sprinted toward Harold. Just as Missy said, the little guy started to run out of steam. He was in a low trot now, his short legs pounding into the sand and making far less headway.

He turned his head to look back, and Quincy stopped and called to him. Harold's body swung around, and he bounded back toward her almost as fast as he'd run through the tent.

Quincy dropped onto the sand and scooped him into her lap.

Moments later, Missy dropped onto the sand beside them. She wheezed and laughed as the dress billowed in the sand around her.

They both caught their breath and gave Harold strokes and scratches. He burrowed happily into Quincy's lap and licked Missy's wrist.

Missy turned to Quincy. "I'm glad we're alone. There's something I need to talk to you about."

Chapter 19

At Some Point You Just Have to Give in and Admit that You're in Love

Missy watched as Quincy rubbed an especially important spot on Harold's chin that made the dog give out a satisfied groan.

"What's on your mind?"

"I've been a little anxious today."

Quincy transferred her hand to Missy's thigh, resting it on top of the silky dress. Missy placed her hand over the top. It was like home.

"I could tell," Quincy said.

"That's why you paused the ceremony at the beginning? To make sure I was okay?"

Quincy nodded, and Missy's heart swelled. She loved that Quincy not only accepted her anxiety, but paid attention to it.

"I got anxious because of something Elaina said, well, and Olivia. Anyway, no one is to blame, I just ended up on a wild goose chase."

Quincy tipped her head and furrowed her brow.

Missy told her the entire story of the mysterious, "Go ask Jack adventure." When she finished, she shrugged her shoulders. "So I never found out."

"I'll tell you everything." Quincy leaned over and gave her a quick kiss. "Olivia, who apparently caused you anxiety today—and I will give her hell for that—actually had a good idea last night. She thought I should call Gina and sort of end that chapter of my life."

"I agree that's a good idea."

"It was. I told Gina, in no uncertain terms, that I didn't want to get back together with her, and that I am so happy to be marrying you."

That was eighty percent of what Missy needed to hear. Could she live with that?

"Then," Quincy continued, "your uncle Jack came over this morning when Olivia and I were hung over as hell. Oh hey!" She stopped to look down at Harold, then back up again. "Harold slept in his crate on his own with the door open."

Missy patted Harold's back with her free hand. "That's because he's a good boy." And he was their good boy. And that counted for a lot, too. Quincy had waited for her to have a dog with. Maybe they were at ninety percent now.

"Anyway, after Jack told me about Gina calling him. By the way, I blocked her number."

"Good job."

"But, I have to apologize to you. Because I told Jack something that I should have told you first."

Missy's chest squeezed. Hope warred with the remaining anxiety that still clung to her. "What did you tell him?"

"That I love you. Well, I don't think I used those words exactly. Maybe I did. I don't remember. But it's what I meant. It's what I meant all along, I just needed to get in touch with myself. You know?"

Missy couldn't speak. So she nodded.

"And I know I should have said it earlier. I'm sorry about that. It won't make sense, but I had to say it to my brothers first. God, that sounds weird."

Missy unraveled her fingers from Quincy's and lifted

her hand to stroke Quincy's cheek. One hundred percent. Maybe one hundred ten.

"It doesn't sound weird at all. I totally get it."

"That's because you get me."

"No. It's because I love you."

Missy looked back at the tent. Music and laughter poured out of it. Their guests had apparently decided not to wait for Missy and Quincy to start the dancing portion of the night. She turned back to her wife.

"You know what I would really like to do?"

Quincy tipped her head. "Go home, snuggle Harold, then put him in his crate and make love on our big king-size bed?"

It was cute how Quincy spoke as if it were a serious question and she didn't already know the answer Missy would give.

"Absolutely."

****

Missy glared at the reporter. She couldn't believe she had the nerve to show up here after Missy had nearly bit the woman's head off outside the airport six months ago. She turned her head and shot her gaze at Myra. This was an invite-only affair. What was she thinking inviting this person?

Beside her, Quincy was unusually talkative. Rather than letting Myra do the intros, she'd taken over that role herself. "Thanks for coming." She shifted back on her feet and looped her intertwined fingers with Missy's.

Missy rubbed her sandal across the grass. She was glad they were using the filming area of the property, rather than their front yard for this little shindig. She didn't want these people, and especially not that one in the front, to invade their private space.

Plus, Harold would bark his head off if they were in what he considered his territory. The thought made her turn to look at him. Out here, on neutral ground, he was chill, lounging at her feet, his pink tongue lolling out of his mouth.

"As you all know," Quincy said, "we haven't given any interviews since our second wedding, despite all your hounding."

Missy couldn't resist a dig. "And all the bullshit, made-up stories in the press."

Quincy took her focus away from the reporters long enough to give her a quick wink. "Yeah. That too."

A short, cute woman standing next to Missy's enemy raised her hand in the air. "Why break your silence now?"

Quincy raised her free hand toward the woman. "Good question. Well, it's because we're changing things up on the show, which is what you should really be talking about, not whether or not we're actually in love."

Missy pulled out her best sarcastic voice. "Oh right. The show! That might be a good thing to actually talk about in the press."

Quincy grinned, and Missy reveled in it. God, she loved that smile. It was a small consolation prize for having to do this press conference. But they were doing something different with the show, and they wanted to make the announcement in a big way to help boost viewership. And, apparently, it might help a deal Uncle Jack was making with a new channel that would skyrocket the show into prime time.

So yeah, they were using these yahoos for their own gain, and that's why Missy had agreed to do it. But she'd gotten an added bonus. With Quincy at her side, Harold at her feet, and a sense of confidence she had never known before, she stood here in front of the press with barely a drop of sweat on her brow.

"Are you in love?" asked the jackass reporter Missy wanted to throttle.

Quincy raised one finger. "I'll tell you what, you all record what I'm about to say regarding the show, and afterwards I'll tell you about our marriage."

A man with messy hair and a wonderful Roman nose shouted out to her, "We're all ears."

Quincy flashed her camera smile at him. How he was still standing after that, Missy had no idea. That smile was a killer. "The show's format is going to change. In addition to me working on one behavior issue with all the dogs during one show, we will have a segment where Missy works with one dog intensively on that behavior. We'll call them the star dog. And I am delighted to announce that the star dog for our first show this season will be our very own Harold."

Dozens of eyes shot to Harold, who shifted on the grass, plopping down on his side to lie in horse position, clearly unimpressed. A few chuckles rang out in the crowd.

"So." Quincy clapped her hands together. "Any questions?"

That damn reporter from the airport piped up. "Yeah. Are you getting a divorce?"

Quincy grabbed Missy's hand again and squeezed. It was the only reason Missy managed to stave off an attack. She bit her lip and let Quincy take that one.

"What part of 'Missy is getting a bigger stake in the show' equals divorce to you, exactly?"

"Are you in love?" The cute woman asked.

"Yes. We sure are."

Quincy just blurting it out like that wasn't part of the

carefully constructed plan they'd created with Myra and Jack, both of whom stood a short distance away and were probably gaping like fish.

But Quincy was gazing into Missy's eyes, and it was clear she didn't care about any plan. She was speaking her truth. And Missy whispered back, just for her, "Yeah. We definitely are."

THE END

Dear Reader,

Thank you for reading a Benna Bos book! If you loved it, thought it was good enough to finish but you have some suggestions, or just want to drop a note to say that you also love dogs, please take a moment to review the book on Amazon or Goodreads. It really, really helps!

Woof!
Benna's Dog

ABOUT THE AUTHOR

Benna Bos is an award-winning author of sapphic fiction with a deep love for curiosity, adventure, and a good story. Benna's tales of love and mystery contain imperfect heroines and impeccable hounds. If you pick up a Benna Bos book, you're guaranteed 3 things: Romance, Mystery, and Dogs.

Her first novel, *Investigating Helen*, won a Lesfic Bard Award and the Carolyn Readers' Choice Award. She followed that up with another romantic suspense and two cozy mysteries starring a tenacious Basset Hound. Her fifth novel, *This Means War*, is a fiery, second chance, enemies-to-lovers romance that explores history, conflict, and the unstoppable attraction between two people no matter how different they appear to be.

Benna lives in San Francisco with her own dog hero and grows an inordinate quantity of plants on her tiny balcony.

Made in the USA
Coppell, TX
21 June 2026

83151407R00132